Oh, Baby!
(A Prescription: Romance! Book)

JILL BLAKE

ISBN: 0-9985387-4-4
ISBN-13: 978-0-9985387-4-7

CONTENTS

CHAPTER 1

Lena Shapiro tapped the home screen on her iPhone. No calls or messages since she'd checked five minutes ago, and the single bar at the top of the screen was still there.

A few steps to the left or right, and she'd get the dreaded *No service* message instead. She'd spent the first ten minutes of the party testing that out, holding the phone out like a dowsing stick in search of decent cell reception.

What she found was this one spot, on the corner of Rachel and Erik's property. And so she'd grabbed a bottle of chilled mineral water to keep the heat at bay, and planted herself here at a table beneath a built-in umbrella.

In the distance, the gray-blue waters of the Pacific glittered beneath the midday sun. Now that the morning mist had burned away, she could see the coastline stretching all the way down to the Santa Monica Pier. There were worse places to be, especially if you had to take call on the Fourth of July.

"Lena, sweetie, what are you doing way over here?"

Lena glanced up and smiled at Rachel, her best friend since college. "Manning the phone. I have a couple post-op patients I'm worried about."

Rachel slid into the nearest empty seat. "I told you, you should have gone into emergency medicine. I do my job and go home. No call, no after-hours headaches."

"Sure," Lena said. "But then I'd have to deal with drunks and drug-seekers and fecal impactions—"

"You win," Rachel laughed. "Have you eaten?"

"Yes, thanks. Erik makes a mean burger."

Rachel smiled and glanced across the lawn toward the built-in outdoor kitchen, where Erik was still flipping burgers and Italian sausages while entertaining their guests. "I have some news."

"Okay…"

Rachel leaned closer and dropped her voice. "I'm pregnant."

"Oh, Rach!" Lena hugged her friend, swallowing a bittersweet mix of joy and envy. "Congratulations. How far along?"

"Twelve weeks. Twins, can you believe it?"

Considering Rachel and Erik had been doing IVF for the past six months, Lena wasn't surprised. "That's wonderful, Rach. How do you feel?"

While Rachel launched into a detailed description of the nausea and swollen boobs and need to pee every five minutes, Lena concentrated on keeping a smile firmly pasted on her lips. If anyone deserved to have a family, it was Rachel. Lena was thrilled for her.

And if the longing that sliced through her felt like a physical pain, Lena was strong enough to ignore it. She'd made her own choice early on. Career first.

What she hadn't realized back then was just how long establishing her career would take. And how much she'd have to sacrifice along the way. She still didn't know if the end result was worth it.

Sure, she was a partner in a busy surgical practice. Vice-Chair of the Department of Surgery at St. Mary's Hospital. Fellow in the American College of Surgeons. She had more patient referrals than she could handle, and so many administrative responsibilities that Rachel told her she should stand in front of a mirror and practice saying *No*.

What Rachel didn't understand was that Lena had no problem saying *No.* At least when it came to her personal life. Which was probably why she was still single and childless at thirty-nine.

"Oh, my God—" Rachel broke off and grabbed Lena's arm. "Don't look!"

"What?" Lena blinked and reflexively followed Rachel's gaze toward the sliding glass doors at the back of the house. "Oh. What's *he* doing here?"

"I told you not to look." Rachel scowled at the newcomer, who was making his way toward the guests clustered around the grill. Either he hadn't seen Lena, or he was choosing to ignore her. "I'm sorry. Erik must have invited him. Are you okay?"

"Fine." Lena forced herself to look away.

"You're better off without him," Rachel said. "The guy's a total prick. In fact, that's what we should call him from now on: *Doctor Prick.*"

"Right," Lena said with a faint smile. *Doctor Prick, the urologist.* "Very funny. Or should I say punny?"

Her phone rang, which was just as well. She didn't feel like rehashing yet another failed relationship. Especially with her well-intentioned but disgustingly happy married-and-pregnant friend.

What was the point, anyway? The pattern of Lena's dating life was always the same, even if the faces changed. Men saw her as a challenge. But at some point, they got tired of competing with her career for attention. When she bailed on one too many dates because of work, their annoyance turned to frustration, which inevitably led to an ultimatum.

Seriously, what was it about the male ego that made guys think she'd choose them over her responsibilities as a surgeon? And why, in today's enlightened society, did she even have to make a choice?

She'd dated Doctor Prick for the last three months. He saw patients, did surgery, took call, just like Lena. At the very least, he should have been more understanding....

Rachel mouthed a silent *See you later* and rose, leaving Lena to deal with her call. It was the emergency room, paging her about a new consult.

Three minutes later, Lena skimmed through the patient's preliminary lab results on her phone, and headed for the house.

She was halfway to the front door when Erik's voice stopped her.

"Lena, wait up!"

She glanced back. Erik's complexion was ruddier than usual. A sheen of sweat coated his face and plastered wisps of thinning reddish hair to his temples.

She slipped the phone into a side pocket of her purse and waited for him to catch up. "Sorry for ducking out," she said. "The ER called with a possible appy."

"I won't keep you, then," he said. "I just have a quick favor to ask. There's a second-year surgical oncology fellow starting with us tomorrow. I need you to take him on."

Her fingers tightened on the shoulder bag. "What do you mean, take him on?"

"Coordinate his rotation at St. Mary's. You're on faculty at CRI, aren't you?"

CRI, or the Cancer Research Institute, was loosely affiliated with St. Mary's, and most of its faculty members were on staff at the hospital.

Lena nodded.

"You've worked with some of their fellows before," Erik said. "So you know the drill. Assign the guy some time in the OR and clinic, supervise his work. Make sure he sees a variety of cases over the next four months."

Lena frowned. She didn't have the time or patience to babysit a trainee. Okay, so maybe a second-year fellow wouldn't slow her down as much as a medical student or resident. But given the choice, she'd rather take call every single night for the next four months, if it got her out of playing mentor to yet another man who thought he walked on water. Some of the fellows who'd passed through St. Mary's had egos even more inflated than the men she'd dated.

"I'll email you his CV tonight," Erik said. "And a packet with the program requirements. You should probably review it before you meet him tomorrow."

She swallowed. "Tomorrow?"

"Is that a problem?"

Yes, she wanted to say. *A huge problem.* But the words stuck in her throat.

Because even though Rachel was right—Lena needed to push back and stop piling more work on her already overflowing plate—she couldn't do it. Not today. And certainly not with Erik, who was still her senior partner and mentor, as well as the hospital's Chief of Surgery. She might be overworked and overwhelmed, but she wasn't stupid.

So she took a deep breath and murmured, "No problem."

"Good." Erik turned to head back to the party. "His name is Adam Sterling," he tossed over his shoulder. "He'll meet you at the office tomorrow at eight."

CHAPTER 2

The following morning, the first thing Lena heard when she entered the office was voices. A deep male rumble, followed by a breathy giggle that belonged to Debbie, their receptionist. The waiting room was empty.

Lena firmed her lips and followed the sound down the hall, to the small staff break room. She pushed open the door and halted, taking in the scene.

Debbie leaned against the counter near the coffee machine, fingers twirling a strand of long blond hair as she gazed up at the man who was propping up a nearby wall.

Lena cleared her throat. "Morning, Debbie."

"Dr. Shapiro!" The receptionist jerked to attention. "Your first appointment canceled. I was just showing Adam—Dr. Sterling—around the office."

"Thank you," Lena said. "I can take it from here."

Debbie nodded. With a parting smile for their visitor, she left them alone.

The man slowly straightened to his full height. "Dr. Shapiro."

Lena sucked in a breath. He was big. A good ten inches taller than her own five foot five. And it wasn't just his height—it was everything. Neck, shoulders, biceps that strained the sleeves of his button-down shirt. And those hands! Did hemostats even come with holes large enough to fit his fingers?

She flushed and watched him approach, resisting the urge to step back.

He stopped about two feet away from her, and his hazel eyes—more green than brown, with a rim of smoky gray—locked on hers.

"Adam Sterling," he said, offering a hand. When she didn't respond, he raised a sandy brow, several shades darker than his hair. "You *were* expecting me, weren't you?"

It was the laughter in his eyes—mirroring the same sentiment in his voice—that broke through her bemusement and got her moving again. She gave him the briefest handshake possible.

"If you'll follow me," she said. "We have a few minutes to go over things."

She turned and headed for her office in the back, hyperaware of his presence behind her.

"Have a seat." She waved toward one of the visitor's chairs and extracted her phone, then slid her shoulder bag into its usual drawer. "I don't know how much Dr. Harding told you—"

She glanced up, and for a moment lost her train of thought. He'd done exactly as instructed. But his relaxed pose brought attention to the rest of him, the parts she hadn't noticed in the break room. His powerful thighs were splayed and clearly outlined in the chinos he wore. The prominent bulge between them drew her gaze and made her forget for a moment that it wasn't polite to stare.

His voice broke her trance. "Dr. Harding said you'd show me the ropes."

Her eyes flew up to meet his. Damn. He'd seen her looking. His lips twitched, as if he were trying to hold back a smile.

She took a deep breath and concentrated on settling into her own chair behind the massive desk. It took a few tries before she was able to log onto her computer, and she blamed that on him, too. His gaze was still trained on her. She could feel it, like the zap of a Bovie cauterizing bleeders. It was surprising there was no smell of sizzling flesh.

She pulled up Erik's email. Not that she needed it for reference, but it gave her something to focus on that wasn't as distracting and intimidating as her visitor.

"I read your CV," she said. "I'm not sure what we can offer you here at St. Mary's that you haven't already seen at Kaiser and the Angeles Clinic."

"I need to get my numbers up," he said. "It's tough when you're competing with senior residents for the most interesting cases. Everyone wants in on the hepatobiliary stuff and a turn with the Da Vinci robot, you know what I mean? Here, I'll get first dibs on all that."

She suppressed an eye-roll. A small community hospital like St. Mary's didn't attract too many complex surgical oncology cases. Those went primarily to larger academic institutions like UCLA and Cedars.

"I'll see what I can do," she said. "Have you met any of our surgeons?"

"Yeah." He named several of her colleagues. "In fact, I'm scrubbing in on a lumpectomy later today with Dr. Harding, and an osteosarcoma first thing tomorrow morning with Dr. Hunter."

"Oh." She blinked. "Okay, then. That's good."

"The opportunity came up. You don't mind, do you?"

"Of course not. Why would I mind?" She glanced at her watch. Crap. Where had the time gone?

"We'll be working together for the next four months," Adam said. "I want to make sure I'm not stepping on any toes."

There was that half-smile again, the one that spiked her pulse and made her breath catch.

"You're not," she said, averting her eyes. She logged into her schedule and scrolled through the list of morning appointments. "But it would help to know what else you have scheduled, so we can coordinate your time in the OR. I assume you'll follow the patients postoperatively?"

"Of course." He pulled his phone from the clip on his belt. "And before surgery, too, for the initial evaluation and treatment planning. You know, for continuity of care."

"I can arrange it for patients in this office, but I can't guarantee you the same access to other outpatient clinics." Just thinking about the logistics was giving her a headache. Why couldn't Erik have saddled someone else in the department with the task?

"That's fine." Adam studied his phone. "I have morning conference on Tuesdays. And I need a couple days a week for research, but I can work those around the clinic schedule."

She nodded. "Dr. Harding and I alternate days in the OR and office. I operate on Tuesdays and Thursdays, while he's in clinic. Monday, Wednesday, and every other Friday, I'm in clinic while he's in the OR. We round on our own post-ops before and after clinic."

There was a knock on the door, and one of the medical assistants leaned her head in. "You have a patient in room one, Dr. Shapiro."

"Thank you." Lena clicked on the patient's chart, and briefly skimmed the chief complaint, vitals, meds, and past medical history. "Looks like a straightforward inguinal hernia." Another click, back to the schedule. "After that, there's a lipoma, umbilical hernia, follow-up on a pilonidal cyst, recurrent diverticulitis, and a consult for a possible lap chole. Looks like you're off the hook today. Unless you're interested in doing more than just oncology cases?"

He shook his head. "I did general surgery for five years. If I never see another pilonidal cyst in my life, that's fine by me. No offense."

Lena bit her tongue. *Arrogant ass.* What did he think he'd be doing a year from now? Unless he planned to go into academic medicine or had the good fortune of taking over a mature practice from an oncology surgeon who was retiring, Dr. I'm-okay-with-never-seeing-another-pilonidal-cyst would see more pilonidal cysts and appys and hernias than he'd ever seen as a resident. It took time to build a specialty surgical practice, and the rent didn't pay itself. Which meant that most subspecialists ended up taking whatever came their way, at least for their first few years in practice.

But it wasn't Lena's job to disillusion him. So she swallowed a caustic response and wished him luck with the lumpectomy.

"Thanks." He rose. "If we're through here, I'll head over to the medical staff office. They have some paperwork for me to sign so I'm officially 'on-boarded'."

Lena froze. "Please tell me you have hospital privileges here."

Until this moment, it hadn't even crossed her mind that he might not, that *she* might have to help him navigate the bureaucracy that determined any physician's right to step foot in St. Mary's.

Impossible. They wouldn't have put him on the OR schedule if he hadn't completed the credentialing process. She hoped.

"You mean it's not automatic?" he asked. Then before she could muster a response, he shook his head and grinned. "Sorry, Lena. Of course I have hospital privileges. They have me on provisional staff to start."

She let out a breath. "It's *Dr. Shapiro.*"

"Sorry?"

"My name," she said. "Dr. Shapiro."

His grin widened, making her flush and wish she'd kept her mouth shut.

"Okay," he said. "So what's on the agenda for tomorrow?"

"I'm in the OR." She glanced back at the computer. "The only thing that might be up your alley is the one o'clock. Colorectal cancer. Patient presented with a bowel obstruction. We'll do a laparascopic colectomy, possible ostomy. You can first-assist."

"Will do," he said. "See you then, *Dr. Shapiro.*"

She watched him saunter out, her eyes sliding down his back to the tapered waist and tight rear.

Heat spread up her neck and cheeks. Grabbing her stethoscope, she pushed back from the desk and stood up. The air conditioning was probably on the fritz again. Third time this year. She'd have to ask Debbie to call building maintenance—

A blast of cold air from the nearby vent gave her pause, cooling her indignation.

Maybe she was having hot flashes. Thirty-nine was young, but not impossible. Which was why she'd frozen her eggs a few years ago, preparing for the possibility that her ovaries would give out before she was ready for kids. So if this *was* the first sign of perimenopause, it wasn't the end of the world.

And it was certainly more palatable than the other explanation that crossed her mind: that she was experiencing the hormonally-fueled fever of lust-at-first-sight. Because *that* would be truly embarrassing. And inappropriate. Especially these days, with all the uproar over sexual misconduct in the workplace. Adam wasn't technically in her employ, but Lena certainly had the power to influence his career—or at least the next few months of his training.

And that wasn't even touching on their age difference. He had to be eight or nine years her junior, given that he'd just finished residency last year. That whole older woman-younger man thing might be trending in Hollywood, but Lena wasn't an actress striving for the illusion of perpetual youth.

At this stage of life, she didn't have time to waste on dead-end relationships. She wanted what her best friend had. Love. Someone to come home to after a crushing day in the OR. A partner with an empathetic ear and enough maturity to accept that the world didn't revolve around him. A man who knew how to cook, or at least didn't mind eating leftovers, and who understood why Lena had to work through the weekend or rush off in the middle of dinner. Someone as eager to start a family as Lena herself was.

She might not have been ready before. But hearing about Rachel's pregnancy was like having the final tumbler fall into place, unlocking the door to her innermost desires.

A family of her own. That's what she wanted. A husband and a child. And if she couldn't have both—because, let's face it, at thirty-nine and a half she couldn't afford to waste time—then she'd choose the child. Before it was too late. Before she was so old and set in her ways that not even the finest medical technology and all the money in the world would be enough to make her dreams come true.

Which meant reassessing her options, and possibly shedding the expectations that had weighed her down for as long as she could remember.

Could she do it? Forgo the conventional route of marriage first and baby later, and do instead what an increasing number of her peers were doing? All she needed was some donor sperm and a few visits to her local fertility clinic.

The hard part would come later: raising a child on her own. And unlike many of the single moms she knew, Lena wouldn't have the support of an extended family. Her father was dead, her sister was too wrapped up in her own dramas to give a damn about anyone else's, and her mother's help would come at too high a cost. She'd rather pay through the nose for childcare than listen to her mother's inexhaustible barrage of criticism.

What she needed to do was carve out some time to go online and research her options. Figure out how to sign up with a sperm bank. Schedule an appointment with her gynecologist.

She'd look into it soon. Maybe even this weekend.

In the meantime, there were patients to see and surgeries to plan, and a way-too-distracting surgical fellow to manage.

CHAPTER 3

The operating room phone rang while Lena was examining the anastomotic staple line for bleeding.

"Call for you, Dr. Shapiro," the circulating nurse said. "It's a Dr. Cohen from Cedars-Sinai."

"I'm almost done here," Lena said, without looking up. "Can you take a message?"

"It's about your mom."

Lena hesitated. Across the table, Adam met her gaze. "I can close," he said, his voice muffled by the surgical mask.

For the last two hours, as they worked in tandem resecting a large sigmoid mass, then performing an anastomosis of the remaining healthy sections of colon, Lena had the chance to observe and admire his technique. He seemed to anticipate her every move, identifying anatomic landmarks with remarkable speed and precision, helping her isolate and mobilize each structure, controlling the bleeders with strategic placement of endoclips before Lena even opened her mouth to ask. Their movements meshed so seamlessly that it felt like they'd been operating together for years.

"Thanks," Lena nodded and stepped away from the table, stripping off her disposable gown and gloves on the way to the wall-mounted phone.

"Dr. Shapiro? Gabe Cohen here. I just wanted to let you know that your mother's surgery went well. She's in the PACU, recovering."

Lena frowned. "My mother had surgery?"

"A total hip replacement. She was brought to the ER this morning with a hip fracture. No one called you?"

"No."

"I'm sorry, I just assumed—" He broke off, and there was the low murmur of voices in the background.

"Is she there?" Lena said. "Can I talk to her?"

"Hold on."

A minute later, Nina Shapiro came on the line. "I'm fine," she said, her voice low and raspy. "No need to fuss."

"What happened?"

"I missed a step and fell. Got a new hip out of it. Are you still at work?"

"Yes." Lena glanced toward the operating table. Even from this distance, she could see the smooth, steady movements of Adam's hands as he sutured the fascial defect. "I have one more case after this, and then post-op rounds. When do visiting hours end?"

"Nine," her mother said. "Don't rush. I'll be here a few days."

Adam caught up with her in the recovery room, where Lena sat at a computer at the nurses' station, finishing up charts.

"Is your mom okay?" he asked.

Lena glanced up and shrugged. "I'll see her tonight. Sorry for bailing. You did a nice job finishing up."

"Thanks." He dropped into a rolling chair beside her. After several minutes of watching her doggedly F2 her way through an op note, he broke the silence. "How far is it from here?"

She blinked. "How far is what?"

"Cedars-Sinai."

"About forty minutes to an hour and a half, depending on traffic," she said. "You've never been there?"

"Once, when I was interviewing for fellowships," he said. "Flew in, spent the day, flew out. Never actually had to drive there."

She frowned. "But you've been in L.A. for, what, a year?"

"Yeah," he said. "And I hate sitting in traffic. I was lucky enough to find sublets close to each hospital I've worked in. Mostly I just walk or bike to work."

No wonder he was in such good shape. Though walking and biking wouldn't account for all that muscle. He probably spent all his spare time in the gym, lifting weights.

She glanced at the wall clock. "Look, I have another case in twenty minutes. So…"

"I can take a hint." He grinned and rose. She was pulling up her next patient's chart when he turned back. "Want some company tonight?"

"Excuse me?"

"We can go visit your mother, and then you can show me around."

Her brow furrowed. "You want a tour of the hospital?"

"Not the hospital. The area around it. Beverly Hills, right?"

"It'll be dark," she said. "You won't see anything."

He shrugged. "Okay, so we'll save Beverly Hills for some other time. How about dinner instead?"

She narrowed her eyes. "Why?"

"Because we both need to eat. And it's dangerous to drive alone late at night. You know how many accidents happen because of people falling asleep behind the wheel?"

"I'm not going to fall asleep behind the wheel."

"Of course not, because I'll be there, keeping you awake with my brilliant conversational skills."

Her mouth fell open. And then she caught the glimmer of humor in his eyes, and blew out a breath. "You're wasting your time."

"Dinner and conversation with a beautiful woman are never a waste of time."

She shook her head. "Now you're just being ridiculous."

A nurse sorting supplies nearby piped up, "If you don't take him up on it, Dr. Shapiro, I will."

The man had the gall to grin and cock his head in Lena's

direction, brows raised, waiting.

"Fine." Lena logged off the computer. "I'll text you when I'm done. We can meet in the parking lot out front."

~

They'd been driving in stop-and-go traffic for half an hour when Adam made another stab at conversation. So far, Lena had offered little besides monosyllabic responses. He'd learned that her mother was widowed, and that there was a sister and two nieces but no other family.

Was she still steamed that he'd railroaded her into taking him along, or was she simply worried about her mom? Either way, he'd promised to provide entertainment, and he didn't want to be accused of slacking on the job.

"So will your sister be there too?" he said. "At the hospital?"

Lena switched lanes. "Doubt it."

"Why?"

"Because she's busy."

His brows shot up. "And you're not?"

Her fingers tightened on the steering wheel. "Zhanna has kids."

"And...?"

"And I don't," Lena bit off.

Adam studied her profile in the fading evening light. "Your mom and sister don't get along?"

"They get along fine. It's just—" she stopped and blew out a breath. "We each have our assigned roles, you know? No matter what else is going on, no matter how old you are, when it comes to dealing with family, you keep slipping back into those roles. I'm the first-born. So..." She glanced at him and shrugged.

"Oh, now I get it," he said. "You're an overachieving perfectionist with the weight of the world on your shoulders."

Her lips quirked. "Maybe not the weight of the world. But responsibility for the family? Absolutely. And since I'm a doctor, anything that's health-related obviously falls within my purview."

"What does your sister Zhanna do while you're taking care of family?"

"I told you, she's a mom."

"How old are her kids?"

"Twelve and eight."

He frowned. "And she can't spare a couple of hours to visit her own mother in the hospital?"

"Adam—"

"Sorry." He raised a placating hand. "None of my business."

She sighed. "What about you? Any siblings?"

"Two sisters," he said. "Both older, married, with kids. Liz—she's the oldest—has two girls and a boy. Amanda has three boys and a fourth on the way."

"Wow. That's...a lot."

"We're a fecund bunch," he grinned. "You should see my parents' house at Thanksgiving and Christmas. Total chaos."

She slid him a speculative look. "You don't have any kids of your own?"

"Nah," he said. "I like being an uncle. But I can't even imagine being a dad. Maybe once I finish fellowship and figure out the rest of my life..."

Lena eased into the right-hand lane to turn onto Beverly Boulevard. "Where to set up shop, you mean?"

"That, and how much to focus on research versus clinical practice," he said. "It's part of the same equation, really. You can do clinical work anywhere. But for research, you need to be where the big players are. Dana Farber, Sloan Kettering, MD Anderson."

"You must have some idea of where you'd want to be..."

"New York," he said without hesitation. "Sloan Kettering. But a lot depends on how things go this year."

"What do you mean?"

"Research," he said. "I'm working on a clinical trial comparing adjuvant immunotherapy in patients with advanced stage melanoma to surgically managed patients with microscopic sentinel node metastases…" He trailed off when he noticed she wasn't paying attention. "Sorry. I forget not everyone's as interested in this stuff as I am."

"I'm interested," Lena said, slowing down as they approached the hospital complex. "But maybe later, after I see my mom?"

"Okay," he said. "I'll hold you to that."

~

It was a shock, seeing her indomitable mother lying pale and still against the white hospital sheets, an IV drip attached to her arm.

Lena hovered beside the bed, wondering whether to sit down or take the opportunity while Nina slept to talk with the evening nurse. The choice was made for her when her mom's eyes fluttered open and a frown creased her brow.

"You came."

"Hi, Ma." Lena touched her mother's blue-veined hand. "How are you feeling?"

"*Ne ploxo*," Nina rasped. "Could be worse."

"Do you need something for pain?"

"No." She shifted and ran her fingers along the control panel of the bed's side rail.

Lena leaned closer. "Here, let me help."

"I'm fine," Nina said sharply, finally finding the right button to raise the head of the bed. "You look tired."

Lena moved the visitor's chair closer to the bed and hung her shoulder bag on the back before sitting down. "I came straight from work."

Nina muttered something under her breath, then winced.

Lena sprang up. "Let me get your nurse."

"I don't need the nurse," her mother said. "You want to be useful? Get me some water."

Lena glanced around. A pink plastic pitcher stood on a nearby tray table. She refilled an empty cup and offered it to her mother. "Dr. Cohen said the surgery went well."

"You saw him?"

"No," Lena said. "He called earlier today, from the PACU, remember?"

"I'm not senile yet," Nina said. After a few sips of water, she handed the cup back. "You should meet him. He's a nice young man. Exactly what you need."

Lena gritted her teeth. "I don't care if he's nice, as long as he did a good job on your hip."

"Don't be so quick to dismiss him. He's a doctor. And he wasn't wearing a wedding ring."

"Neither do most of the married surgeons I work with," Lena said. Pulling the rolling tray table closer to the bed, she spent several minutes arranging the water pitcher, cup, and a box of tissues so they'd be within easy reach.

Nina jerked the top sheet higher up over her chest. "You want to end up old and alone?"

"Ma—"

"I'll have him call you when he stops by tomorrow."

"Fine," Lena said. "He can update me on how you're doing and what the plans are for rehab."

"I know what the plans are. And I can tell you right now, I'm not going to any facility."

Lena took a slow, deep breath. "If the doctor says—"

"Whatever he says, I'm going home. And that's that."

"Fine. We'll readdress it once you're up and around, closer to discharge. In the meantime, can I get you anything else? To make you more comfortable while you're here?"

"I could use some clothes from home. A robe, slippers…"

Lena nodded. "Anything else?"

"My reading glasses," her mother said. "I left them on the kitchen counter."

"I should probably get going, then." Lena glanced at her watch.

"No rush," Nina said. "It can wait till tomorrow."

"I'm in clinic all day tomorrow. I won't be able to get here until evening."

Her mother flicked a dismissive hand. "I've waited this long. Another day won't kill me. Have you eaten?"

"Not yet."

"So eat. What are you waiting for? Send the nurse in on your way out. I'll take some of that pain medicine now."

"Okay." Lena leaned down and kissed her mother's cheek. "I'll see you tomorrow."

~

Adam sensed her presence the moment Lena stepped into the visitor lounge. He looked up and rose, putting away his phone. "How'd it go?"

Lena blew out a breath. "Fine. She's back to her usual ornery self."

"That's a good thing, right?"

"Right." Lena's fingers tightened on the shoulder strap of her bag. "Ready to go?"

He swept his arm toward the door. "After you."

They rode the elevator down in silence. While Lena stared at the wall panel display that showed each floor number as it slid by, Adam studied her face.

On the surface, her features were quite ordinary. Black hair pulled into a neat coil at the back of her head, brown eyes framed by thick lashes, lips slicked with a hint of clear gloss.

He'd dated women far more beautiful, some who even made a living off their looks. And yet the memory of those women left him cold.

Lena, on the other hand, made him feel anything but cold.

There was something about her, a barely-contained energy, that drew him. He'd sensed it the moment they met, when she'd walked in on him flirting with the receptionist. The way she looked at him, lips tight, nostrils flaring. The flash of heat in her eyes before she deliberately blanked her expression and spoke in a carefully modulated tone.

But she couldn't completely suppress the energy that crackled behind that bland facade. It came out in brief bursts,

like static electricity. Like that little power play in her office—
"It's *Dr. Shapiro*," she'd said, all cool and prim, as if she hadn't
just ogled his crotch. He'd almost burst out laughing right then
and there.

The contrast between her icy veneer and the fire beneath it
made him want to egg her on. He felt like a kindergartner,
tugging a girl's pigtails. How far could he push her before she
unleashed all that bottled-up energy?

The elevator doors opened, and a couple who looked like
they were in their seventies entered.

Adam stepped closer to Lena, to give the newcomers room.
His lips twitched when Lena sidled away from him,
maintaining the same distance between them. The movement
brought her flush against the far wall of the elevator.

What would she do if he shifted again, into her personal
space? Would she turn on him and demand to know what the
hell he was doing? Threaten to report him to the director of his
training program for breaching professional boundaries?

That thought, along with the presence of witnesses, was
enough to keep him rooted in place.

But there was nothing to keep his eyes from wandering.
They slid down Lena's body, cataloging the subtle curves that
she usually kept hidden beneath androgynous hospital scrubs
and a baggy white coat.

Tonight she wore a fitted black pantsuit that did nothing to
hide her femininity. A lacy camisole peeked from beneath the
jacket, skimming the tops of her breasts. Adam imagined
flicking open the two buttons that secured the jacket. Sliding it
off. Wrapping his hands around her waist and—

The elevator doors opened, cutting off his fantasy. Good
thing, too. A few more seconds, and he wouldn't have been
able to walk without giving away the direction of his thoughts.

The elderly couple exited. Lena followed without even
glancing at Adam. He caught up with her in a few strides and
kept pace as she headed for the exit, their footsteps echoing
across the marble lobby floor.

Outside, there was a definite nip in the air as they made

their way across the floodlit courtyard toward the parking structure.

"Where to now?" he said.

She clicked the fob to unlock the car. "There's a ton of restaurants between here and Santa Monica. Chinese, Thai, French, Italian. What are you in the mood for?"

He nearly groaned. *Food, you moron. She's talking about food.*

"Any place with quick service," he said. "I don't know about you, but I'm starving."

~

Over skewers of beef and lamb dipped in hot chili oil, Lena listened as Adam described his research. She nodded and asked the occasional follow-up question, but found herself getting repeatedly distracted. Was it the light, or did his eyes really shift color when he became more animated?

"We're making progress," he said. "But it's slow. I'm hoping to pick up the pace in November."

"What happens then?"

"I start my next rotation." He grinned. "No clinical work. Just four months of pure research."

"No clinical work for *four months?*" She stared at him. Was this the same man who'd practically salivated over the idea of getting first dibs in the OR? "Aren't you worried you'll get rusty if you take that much time off?"

"It's not time off," he said. "I'll be doing research. Besides, CRI has an agreement with St. Mary's that allows fellows to moonlight. I'll probably do a few shifts to keep up my skills."

Well, at least that made some sense. She'd witnessed his skills in the OR. St. Mary's would be lucky to have him, even if it was only for a few more months.

She resumed eating. Several minutes later, she realized she'd lost track of the conversation yet again.

"The thing about Westport," he was saying, "is that no one outside of Connecticut's ever heard of it. And people from outside the U.S. are like, Connecti-*what?* So in the end, I usually say I'm from just outside New York, because everyone knows New York, right?"

She paused, chopsticks halfway to her mouth. "I've never actually been to New York."

"You're kidding," he said. "*Never?*"

"We didn't have the money growing up. And once there was money, I didn't have the time."

"But...what about vacations?"

"Welcome to my world. It's called private practice. You eat what you kill—or rather, don't kill." She smiled and shrugged. "I've taken a few weekends here and there. Santa Barbara, San Diego. Local stuff."

If his brows climbed any higher, they'd disappear from his face. "Damn," he said. "We've got to broaden your horizons."

Lena dragged the last piece of steamed broccoli through a puddle of sauce. She was loathe to admit it, but Adam had touched on a sore point. Travel was something that other people did. Classmates who didn't need full scholarships to Harvard-Westlake, who skied every winter in Aspen and Telluride, and split their summers between Europe and Hawaii. College roommates who could spare a gap year to explore Indonesia or climb Kilimanjaro.

In school, and later in residency, she'd promised herself: someday she would see the world. Or at least some small portion of it beyond California.

And now, here she was, a decade later, on the cusp of a major life change that would make travel next to impossible. At least for a few more years, unless she planned something now, before getting pregnant. After her mother recovered from surgery. After Adam was no longer her responsibility.

Their waiter returned to clear the table. "Dessert?"

Lena glanced around, surprised to find the restaurant had emptied out, leaving her and Adam the lone stragglers.

"Not for me," she said.

Adam declined as well.

When the bill came, he insisted on paying. "Only fair, since I invited myself along," he said, with a smile that made her breath catch. "You can pick up the tab next time if you want."

While he thanked the waitstaff and left a generous tip, she mulled over his assumption that there would be a next time.

His fingers brushed the small of her back as he guided her out the door. She flushed, feeling the warmth spreading from the point of contact to encompass every erogenous zone she possessed.

"Want me to drive?" he said.

"No, I've got it, thanks."

Traffic flowed smoothly, and they reached Santa Monica in half the time it would have taken during rush hour.

"Would you mind dropping me off at home?" he asked, as they turned off the freeway. "I'm a few blocks down from the hospital."

He gave her the address, and she raised a brow. "Nice."

"It's worked out so far," he said. "Are you in Santa Monica too?"

"Venice. It's still within a half hour drive from the hospital, so I can sleep in my own bed if call isn't busy." She turned onto his street. "But it's certainly not as convenient as this."

She pulled into an empty parking space halfway down the block.

"That's me." He pointed toward a small bungalow several doors away. "Want to come in?"

"Thanks, but..." She shook her head. "It's late. I need to get home."

He unbuckled his seatbelt. "Next time?"

There it was again, that less-than-subtle hint of future expectations. Her stomach clenched with a disconcerting mix of excitement and trepidation. She shouldn't encourage him. They worked together. She was his preceptor. Anything personal between them, however casual, fell under the heading of Bad Idea.

Besides, they were at completely different stages of life. She was looking for a baby daddy, even if he came in the form of a test tube. In six months, she'd be forty. She didn't have time to play around. Whereas Adam wasn't even in the contemplation stage for parenthood. He'd flat out said he wasn't interested.

They were just as far apart in terms of career. She'd worked her ass off for nearly a decade, building up a surgical practice in L.A. Adam was barely out of the starting gate. And who knew where he'd end up? From the sound of it, his top choices were oncology research opportunities on the opposite coast.

She should put an end to this thing brewing between them—whatever it was—right now.

"Adam…"

"Yes?"

"Thanks for tonight," she said. "For coming with me, I mean. And dinner."

"My pleasure." He smiled and reached for the door handle. "Don't forget, you still owe me a tour of Beverly Hills."

"Um, about that…you'd be better off taking one of those organized tours. You know, the big red hop-on/hop-off double-deckers?"

He shifted back to face her. "Are you trying to weasel out of playing tour guide?"

"Absolutely. I don't know the area that well—"

"But you grew up here, right?"

"In West Hollywood," she said. "And even that's changed since I've lived there."

"I see." He paused, then shrugged. "No problem. We can explore L.A. together."

She sighed. "Adam—"

"I'll see you tomorrow at the hospital. You round on your post-ops before clinic, right?"

She blinked. "Yes. But you don't have to—"

"Six-thirty?"

"Uh, okay. Sure."

She watched him climb out of the car and make his way down the street toward the bungalow he'd pointed out earlier. A motion-activated light illuminated his profile as he turned at the door and lifted a hand in farewell before disappearing inside.

She waited until her pulse slowed to normal, then put the

CHAPTER 4

Adam was already on the med-surg floor when Lena arrived at six-thirty the following morning.

His smile was too bright for her to handle this early. Especially after she'd spent a restless night contemplating the wisdom of seeing him again.

Sometime around one in the morning, it occurred to her that all she needed to do was find a colleague willing to take Adam on. It might take a while, and Erik would probably be pissed over having his authority undermined. But she'd much rather deal with Erik's anger than endure four more months of temptation and guilt. Had she known how much of a menace Adam would be to her equilibrium, she would never have agreed to the assignment in the first place.

Pawning him off on someone else would solve the problem. Out of sight and all that. And if by chance Adam still managed to sneak his way into her thoughts, at least she wouldn't be risking professional censure for crossing some ethical line at work.

She rounded the nurses' station to access the first available computer.

"Morning," Adam said, following.

She returned the greeting without looking up.

"I just saw Mrs. Patel," he said. "Considering it's her first day out from surgery, she's doing really well. Afebrile, vital signs are stable. Her pain and nausea are well controlled."

"Mm-hm," Lena said, logging into the medical record.

"She's getting Zofran for the nausea," Adam continued. "Gabapentin, Toradol, and a PCA pump for the pain. Lovenox for DVT prophylaxis."

He stepped closer, into Lena's personal space, the sleeve of his white coat brushing her arm. His hand hovered over hers on the computer mouse. "May I?"

She closed her eyes for a moment as the scent of his aftershave—a hint of bergamot and macadamia—teased her senses. His body radiated enough heat to spike her temperature a degree or two. She swallowed and moved out of his way.

"There's no flatus or bowel sounds yet," he said, clicking through the patient's chart, "though she is tolerating sips of clears. The JPs are draining about 50 cc's of serosanguineous fluid per shift. Her urine's clear. Looks like she put out nine hundred cc's overnight. I think we can d/c the foley and do a voiding trial."

Lena nodded, resigning herself to Adam's continued presence by her side. At least until she finished her morning rounds. "Has she been out of bed?"

"Once, to the chair and back. You want to go see her?"

"Yes," Lena said. "Which room?"

"Come, I'll show you."

"You don't need to—" she started, but he was already heading down the hall.

It took another forty minutes to see her remaining post-op patients. Adam saved her a good twenty minutes and a whole lot of aggravation by completing the progress notes ahead of time. All she had to do was skim his notes and add a pro forma attestation confirming the findings, assessment, and plan.

"So, boss," Adam said after she signed off on the last chart. "Did I pass?"

She frowned. "I'm not grading you."

"I know." The hint of mischief in his eyes belied his pious

expression. "But maybe you'll write me a good recommendation letter…"

She froze. "You need a recommendation letter? From *me?*"

"Well, yeah," he said, lips twitching. "I'm not sure Sloan Kettering would be too impressed if the letter came from *me.*"

Was that what last night was all about? Cozying up to her, to ensure that she gave him a positive evaluation? All that talk of exploring L.A. together…was it just a ploy to gain her cooperation in helping him with his career? How humiliating. To have so completely misread the situation, assuming an attraction that might exist only in her head.

Unless…

She looked at him, trying to see past the hot-enough-to-cause-palpitations body, past the flash of his dimples, past the grin that seemed to invite her to join in on the joke.

Even if he wasn't faking it, she was in big trouble.

Because professional integrity worked both ways. People might say that *she* was the one taking advantage of her position to pursue Adam. The perception of impropriety could be almost as damaging as the reality.

Either way, she was screwed.

"I have to go," she said. "Thanks for your help this morning."

Without waiting for his response, she headed for the elevators.

At least she hadn't done anything that couldn't be undone. Thank God she'd simply dropped Adam off last night, instead of accepting his invitation to come inside. How much worse would it have been if she'd taken him up on the offer?

She shuddered.

No question about it. She needed to dump Adam in someone else's lap. The sooner that happened, the better.

~

Friday passed in a blur of appointments. A few last-minute add-ons tacked onto the end of her schedule kept her busy well after the receptionists and all but one of the back office staff left for the day.

"I'm about to head out," the lone remaining medical assistant said, popping her head in as Lena settled in front of her desktop computer. "Do you need anything before I go?"

Lena glanced up from an inbox bursting with new messages. "No, thanks. I appreciate your staying late."

"No prob. Have a good weekend, Dr. Shapiro."

Lena slogged through the most urgent patient calls, emails, and results. She still had evening rounds to get through before signing out to the surgeon who was covering the weekend.

As she headed for the hospital, Lena skimmed through the missed messages on her phone. Several of the colleagues she'd contacted earlier in the day about Adam's preceptorship declined, citing an assortment of professional and personal obligations. There were still a few she hadn't heard back from, but she wasn't holding her breath.

This weekend, she'd have to cast a wider net.

But the following day, her good intentions got buried beneath an avalanche of other things requiring her attention. First and foremost, her mother.

CHAPTER 5

The case manager pulled Lena aside on Saturday afternoon, while Nina worked with the physical therapist.

"We need to discuss discharge planning," the woman said. "The physical therapist recommends that your mother go to a skilled nursing facility for rehab, and Dr. Cohen agrees. But your mom's refusing. She says she wants to go home. Maybe if you talked with her...?"

Lena shook her head. "I've tried. Did the doctor say when she'll be ready for discharge?"

The case manager checked her notes. "Maybe tomorrow. Monday at the latest."

Which gave Lena just a day or two to prepare. Not much time, especially if her mother remained adamant about going straight home.

"She's going to need a lot of help," the case manager warned. "Home health only covers so much. And the physical therapy at a SNF is far better than anything she's likely to get at home."

"We could hire someone privately..."

"It's not just about the PT," the case manager said. "Your mom needs someone with her around the clock for safety. She still needs help with transfers and ADLs like bathing."

Lena took out her phone and started making a list. "If you can recommend some local agencies, I'll call and see about getting a caregiver."

"Your mom also mentioned some stairs."

Lena stopped typing and looked up. "Is that a problem?"

"It can be, right after a hip replacement. Let's see…" The case manager leafed through several pages on her clipboard. "There are eighteen steps from the ground floor to the bedroom. And no walk-in showers, only bathtubs. If your mom was stronger, more stable on her feet, it might work. But right now? I really think you should talk to her, see if you can convince her to go to a SNF."

Lena sighed. "Let me talk with my sister first. Maybe we can figure out a way to make it work at home. Put a hospital bed in the living room…"

"It's your call," the case manager said. "But realize that either way, we'll need time to set things up, whether it's a transfer to a facility, or arranging home health and ordering equipment."

"I understand."

The case manager handed her a printed sheet. "These are the agencies we use. Most of them also offer private pay nurses and home health aides. Let me know what you decide. Here's my card. I'm here until five."

Lena thanked her, then took a deep breath and pulled out her phone.

"Sorry, but I can't help," her sister said, after Lena laid out the options. "You need to find someone else to babysit her."

Lena closed her eyes and pinched the bridge of her nose. "I'm trying, Zhanna. But until it's all arranged—"

"Why don't *you* stay with her until you find someone?"

"Because I have a job."

"So do I," Zhanna retorted. "The difference is I don't get paid to do it."

"You have a husband," Lena said. "And a nanny. Surely between the two of them, they can manage the kids for a few days."

"Patrick is on a jobsite," Zhanna said. "And Rosa can't handle the kids by herself. They're at different camps this week, so we both need to do the driving—"

"That's what, an hour or two a day?" Lena said. "And there's always carpool, and Uber for kids."

"I'm not trusting my kids to some stranger—"

"It's a day or two of your time, Zhanna. That's all I'm asking. To help Mom."

"Why can't she go to a nursing facility?"

"Because she doesn't want to," Lena said. "She wants to go home."

"Well, tell her she can't. Tell her she needs to follow doctor's orders and go someplace where they can provide the care she needs."

Lena glanced up as her mother returned to the room, slowly pushing the walker while the physical therapist followed a step behind, arm outstretched to safeguard against falls.

"Never mind," Lena said. "I'll deal with it."

Stupid, to be so disappointed. Especially when Zhanna was simply doing what she always did: washing her hands of all responsibility, because she knew that Lena would pick up the slack and take care of everything.

Lena tucked away the phone and moved to help her mother back into bed. "How did it go, Ma?"

Nina grunted and dismissed the therapist. "Who was that on the phone?"

"Zhanna. She says hello."

"What, she couldn't tell me herself?"

Lena sighed. "You could always pick up the phone and call her. You want me to dial?"

"Later." She yanked up the covers that Lena had been trying to rearrange. "You missed Dr. Cohen. He came by earlier."

"I talked with him on the phone yesterday." Lena straightened and stepped away from the bed. "He's really concerned about you going home. The case manager says—"

"That woman." Nina flapped her hand, as if shooing away

an insect. "What does she know? You remember when Masha Mikhailovna had her knee replaced and stayed in one of those places? Terrible, terrible. One nurse for twenty, thirty patients. And those nursing assistants? Worse than useless. A person could die waiting for some nitroglycerin and they wouldn't discover the body for hours."

"Then it's a good thing you don't need nitroglycerin, isn't it?" Lena said.

Nina frowned. "I'm not going to a facility."

Lena waited a few beats, but her mother remained stubbornly silent.

"Fine. I need to go and make some calls." She kissed her mother goodbye. "I'll see you tomorrow."

~

Eight candidates, and only one even vaguely qualified and willing to move in by Monday.

Lena rose from her mother's kitchen table and stretched to relieve the tightness in her lower back.

She'd missed her usual morning run and begged off a girls' brunch with Rachel in order to spend the day preparing for her mother's arrival.

Hospital bed—check.

Portable commode—check.

Bamboo screen, purchased at some garage sale when the family was still renting a one-bedroom, now repurposed to provide some privacy in the ground floor living room where her mother would sleep until she could manage stairs—check.

Freshly stocked refrigerator, clean linen, a pile of bestsellers in Russian translation on the end table. Check, check, check.

She'd rolled up and put away the loose rugs, tacked down power cords to minimize the risk of tripping, and browbeaten Zhanna into bringing their mother home from the hospital—because no, Lena couldn't take Monday off to do the chauffeuring, not with her clinic schedule already packed to capacity. But she could take her nieces for a weekend, so

Zhanna and her husband could escape to their house in Lake Arrowhead to—in Zhanna's words—"get their marriage back on track". Whatever that meant. Lena didn't ask, and Zhanna didn't elaborate.

The caregiver Lena hired sight unseen promised to show up by noon the following day. Which meant a quick trip to the local grocery for a box of *ptichye moloko* to bring to Masha Mikhailovna, who lived across the street, because someone had to let the caregiver in if Zhanna was running late.

The only thing still pending was the physical therapist, because the home health agency hadn't gotten back to Lena about availability. She made a note to call them again in the morning, between patients.

It wasn't until she fell into bed, exhausted, that she remembered the other item on her to-do list. The one she hadn't gotten around to tackling.

Adam.

Damn. He was still her responsibility. And she'd have to face him first thing tomorrow morning.

She fell asleep, dreaming of hazel eyes and peek-a-boo dimples and an alarm clock that kept ringing, no matter how many times she pressed snooze.

CHAPTER 6

Adam had already seen her patients—and his—by the time she dragged herself in the next morning.

"Rough night?" he asked.

Apparently her under-eye concealer didn't live up to its promise. She shrugged and glanced at the signout list on her phone. "Who's first?"

He took the hint and ran through the list with her.

Later, between patients, he stopped by her office and knocked on the open door. "Got a minute?"

Lena looked up from the chart she was reviewing. "Sure. What's up?"

"I saw an interesting case that I wanted to run by you." He dropped into the visitor's chair and gave her the sixty-second version. "So what do you think? PET scan?"

"PET scan," she agreed. "But you knew that coming in. Do you want to tell me why you're really here?"

"Busted." He flashed his dimples, then got serious again. "How's your mom?"

Lena stiffened. "Fine, thanks. They're discharging her home today."

"So soon? Is she ready for that?"

"She refused the SNF. So…" Lena shrugged. "We'll see. I

did what I could this weekend, setting things up for her."

"You should have called me."

"Why?"

"Because I wasn't doing anything," he said. "There's only so many hours you can spend at the gym. Believe me, I would have been happy to help."

Her mouth fell open. He had to be joking. Lena practically had to bribe her sister to do the absolute minimum. An entire weekend of babysitting in exchange for one lousy ride. And Zhanna was *family*.

Adam was barely even an acquaintance. Sure, they'd shared some patients. And swapped a few childhood memories over an impromptu meal. But whatever illusion of closeness that might have created was just that: an illusion. Their relationship, if she could even call it that, started and ended with his stint at St. Mary's. And if she had her way, Adam would become someone else's responsibility well before his rotation was over.

"Dr. Shapiro?" the medical assistant interrupted before Lena could think of an appropriate response. "Your next patient's in room two."

"Thanks." Lena rose and hesitated. "Adam…"

"Yes?"

"Let me know when the PET scan results are in."

He gave her a look that made her wish she were braver. Or at least more willing to bend, if not break, the rules.

~

Adam scanned the OR schedule for the rest of the week. There were a handful of cases he wanted to scrub in on. He jotted down the names of the attending surgeons. St. Mary's was small enough that he'd met most of them already, and he had no qualms about approaching them directly. At a larger institution, where the hierarchy was more rigid, he would have asked his faculty advisor to manage the logistics. But Lena was busy and had enough to worry about. And frankly, Adam hadn't gotten this far in his career by sitting back and waiting for an invitation.

Half an hour and a handful of phone calls later, he headed to Lena's office.

She was seated at her desk, fingers flying across a keyboard, eyes glued to the computer screen. Her white coat hung over the back of her chair, leaving her in a sleeveless silk blouse that dipped between her breasts and did little to hide the effects of the air conditioning.

He forced his eyes back to her face and cleared his throat. "Can I interest you in a lunch break?"

She looked up, blinking. "I usually work through lunch."

"How about I grab us something from the cafeteria and bring it here?"

"I'm not hungry." She turned back to the screen. "Thanks."

Adam studied her. So much for making progress. At dinner last week, he'd seen a glimmer of the woman behind the frosty veneer, and he liked that woman.

She was bright and funny and her eyes didn't glaze over when he talked shop. He didn't have to tell her why opening up a noxious pus-filled pilonidal cyst was his least favorite procedure. She was a surgeon. She understood him at a word and no doubt agreed with the sentiment. He was free to pepper his speech with medical shorthand without having to pause every third word to explain a term that was second nature to anyone in the field.

He might not have appreciated having that connection in the past, when the grind of studying and working eighty to a hundred hours a week made him long for mindless conversation that had nothing to do with medicine. Or better yet, a mindless fuck that didn't require conversation.

But now, with the end of his fellowship training in sight, and the second-hand wisdom he'd gleaned from friends and colleagues whose relationships failed thanks to the demands of the job, he was starting to rethink his earlier stance. It was probably a good thing if the woman sitting across the dinner table or sharing his pillow understood his passion for the work that consumed most of his waking hours.

Which was why Lena was perfect. She *shared* that passion. Adam saw proof of that in every interaction she had with patients.

His gaze dropped again to her breasts and he grinned. Smart, passionate, *and* the owner of a gorgeous pair of tits.

If she made him wait much longer, he'd have a serious case of blue-balls on his hands.

He scanned the room for inspiration. And there it was, sitting atop a pile of paperwork on the corner of her credenza.

"Is that the latest *JACM?*" He moved closer and reached for the journal. "You don't mind, do you? I'll just sit here—" he waved toward a small love seat along the far wall, tucked between a bookcase and an end table "—and read quietly."

"Help yourself," she said drily. "But don't you have an office or something you can use?"

"Sure." He shed his white coat and draped it over one of the visitor's chairs, then sauntered across the room, where he toed off his shoes and proceeded to make himself comfortable. Or as comfortable as he could get, considering the love seat fell far short of his six foot three inches, and Lena was still staring at him, her expression now more irritated than bemused. "But it's the size of a supply closet, and there are three other fellows sharing the space. So…"

"Do you always get this chummy with your attendings?"

Ooh, now she was pulling rank. He hid a grin. "I wouldn't call breathing the same air on opposite sides of the room *chummy.*"

Silence. He opened the journal and perused the table of contents.

"Dr. Harding's in the OR today," she said. "You can use his office down the hall. I'm sure he wouldn't mind."

He looked at her. "Did I do something to piss you off?"

She fiddled with her computer mouse. "No."

"Then what's going on?" He dropped all pretense of reading and sat up. "I thought we had a good time last week. Now it sounds like you're trying to get rid of me."

A flush spread across her face. "Look, Adam, I think you're

a terrific surgeon, with a really promising career."

"But…?"

"But nothing," she said. "We work well together. Let's leave it at that, okay?"

"Why?" He shoved his feet back into his shoes and stood, tossing aside the journal. And then an unwelcome thought occurred to him. "Are you seeing someone?"

"No."

"Okay, then." He crossed the room, stopping right in front of her desk. "Neither am I. So I don't see the problem in us having an occasional meal together."

She blew out an exasperated breath. "I told you, I don't eat lunch."

"So make it dinner. Tonight, after we're both done with patients."

"I can't."

He narrowed his eyes. "Can't, or won't?"

"Won't." Her eyes met his, then dropped back to her computer screen. "Look, you said you needed a recommendation letter."

"What?"

"After your rotation here ends," she said. "That's fine. I'm more than happy to write it. But I can't do lunch or dinner or anything else. It would be unethical for me to have a personal relationship with someone whose work I'm technically supposed to supervise and evaluate."

Really? *That* was her excuse for avoiding him?

He stared at the top of her bent head. "Fine."

She glanced at him, as if startled by his easy capitulation. "Fine?"

"Yes." He nodded and headed for the door. "See you tomorrow."

"Tomorrow?"

"Yep. I'm scrubbing in on a Whipple this afternoon." He checked his watch. "But that's not till one. Still plenty of time for lunch. Call me if you change your mind."

~

Of course she didn't call. Adam didn't expect her to. That would have been too easy.

And Lena was anything but easy. Maybe, in some perverse way, that fed his attraction to her. The fact that she didn't respond as expected, despite the spark of interest in her eyes.

But then, he was a man who relished a challenge.

The way he saw it, he had two choices.

He could wait until his rotation ended before pursuing Lena. That would eliminate the potential conflict of interest she seemed so concerned about. But, damn, what a waste of patience and cold water that would be.

Besides, he wouldn't be at St. Mary's long. Four months on his current rotation and then another four of doing research and possibly some moonlighting. After that, it was back to the East coast for his final rotation, where he'd get an inside look at his top choice for a post-fellowship position.

So, option number two: find another advisor. Get rid of the obstacle Lena claimed stood in the way of pursuing something a lot more interesting than a simple working relationship.

The opportunity came up that very afternoon. The surgeon he was assisting in the Whipple procedure happened to be the Chief of Surgery himself, Erik Harding. Who better to approach with his request?

CHAPTER 7

The following day, Erik cornered Lena in the doctors' lounge while she was refueling between cases.

"Is there a problem I need to know about?" he said.

"What?" She turned, cup in hand, and barely missed spilling coffee on his shoes.

"You and Sterling. The new fellow. What's going on?"

She reached for a napkin and concentrated on wiping a few stray drops from her fingers. "Nothing. We just finished a melanoma excision. Why?"

"He came to me yesterday and asked for a new advisor."

"*What?*" No wonder Adam had been eyeing her for the last hour, as if waiting for her to say something other than, *Looks clear. Let's suction and close.*

Erik glanced around. It was a quarter past three, and the lounge was nearly empty. A doctor in a rumpled white coat and at least two days' growth of beard napped on one of the couches in front of a large screen television blaring CNN. Another sat in the corner, hunched over his phone, wolfing down a sorry-looking sandwich.

Erik ushered her toward an unoccupied seating area.

"He tried to be slick," Erik said, dropping into an armchair. "Admired my technique. Said what a privilege and honor it would be if I'd allow him to work more closely with me, so he could really learn from all my years of surgical experience. Jesus. Is that what they teach in med school these days? Brown-nosing 101?"

Lena bit her lip. "What did you tell him?"

"I said I'd think about it." He sighed and leaned forward, resting his elbows on his spread knees, hands clasped. "Rachel's been on my case to delegate more. If this is what happens when I try…"

Lena hunched her shoulders. "I'm sorry."

"Just tell me if there's anything I need to know before I take him on. I don't want any more surprises." Erik stared hard at her. "If there's an issue—"

"There are no issues. Adam's good. *Really* good. He knows what he's doing. He's thorough, hardworking. Patients seem to love him…" She trailed off as Erik's lips twitched.

"And this," he said, "is why you tried to get rid of him?"

"Ah." She set down her coffee. "You heard about that?"

"St. Mary's isn't that big," he said. "Word gets around."

She braced herself for an interrogation that never came. The silence lengthened.

In the background, the newscaster provided updates on the wildfires sweeping through central and northern California. At the mention of evacuations in Santa Barbara, Erik stirred and glanced at the TV.

"Do you have someone there?" Lena said once the broadcast went to commercial.

"My wife—*ex*-wife." He rubbed the back of his neck. "The kids are down here with me for the summer."

"Are you worried about your ex?"

"If anything goes wrong, I'm sure I'll be the first to hear about it." He straightened and glanced at his watch. "Anyway, about Sterling. I'll sort his schedule, and he can work with me in clinic."

"Thank you."

"You're not totally off the hook, Lena. I'm still assigning him to your oncology cases. I trust that won't be a problem?"

She swallowed. "No problem."

She'd told Erik that last week, too. And yet here they were.

At least this time her exposure to Adam would be limited. And the headache of scheduling and evaluating his work would be Erik's.

"I need to get back to the office," Erik said, getting up. "One more thing…"

"Yes?"

"Rachel said to call her if you need any help with your mother."

"Oh." Lena let out a breath. "Thanks."

He nodded and left.

Lena settled back in her armchair and closed her eyes. She'd checked on her mom last night, driving to West Hollywood for a brief visit. The caregiver assured Lena that everything was under control. And her mom did sound pretty chipper on the phone earlier today. Maybe her insistence on recuperating at home wasn't so crazy after all.

Her cell phone vibrated. Lena startled awake, disoriented.

"Dr. Shapiro?" It was one of the nurses in the pre-op holding area. "The anesthesiologist was wondering if you'd be much longer?"

She glanced at the wall clock. *Damn.* "I'm on my way."

Downing the now-cold coffee in three gulps, Lena headed for the surgical suite.

~

"Double shot caffè latte with two sugars," Adam said, setting the cup on the counter beside her.

Lena looked up from her patient's chart. Her gaze zeroed in on the coffee before shifting to Adam—moving up past the unbuttoned white coat and casual slacks, the thin striped Oxford shirt with its open collar, the strong tanned neck and square clean-shaven jaw, until she reached his eyes and felt her breath catch at the heat in his expression.

Thank goodness she was already sitting, because at that

moment she wasn't sure her legs would support her. The sound of phones ringing and medical staff going about their business receded. All she could hear was the pounding of her own heart.

She averted her gaze and reached for the cup. The first hit of caffeine surged through her system, dispersing the lingering fatigue from a sleepless night on call.

"Mm," she sighed. "Thanks."

"My pleasure."

From the corner of her eye, Lena saw him pull the flaps of his white coat together and button it up. She took another sip. "How'd you know what I like?"

"Lucky guess," he said.

She raised a brow.

He grinned and shrugged. "Plus I bribed the nurses. They know everything."

Before Lena could decide whether to be flattered or annoyed that he'd gone to the trouble, several of the night shift nurses filed out of the break room, talking and laughing.

"Thanks for breakfast," one of them called to Adam, prompting the rest to echo her words as they headed for the elevators.

Lena waited until the elevator doors closed behind them. "Breakfast?"

"Free food," he said. "Works every time. You hungry?"

She shook her head and took another sip of coffee. "Why are you really here?"

"To see my post-ops," he said. "And to find out when you're available for dinner."

Ah. She'd wondered if he would make another move. Why else would he have gone to Erik, asking to be reassigned?

Now that she was no longer Adam's preceptor, he probably expected the rest would be a slam-dunk. Dinner, wine, a little mood lighting and soft music to set the tone. Then sex. Hot, wall-banging, can't-wait-for-it sex.

She sucked in a breath and flicked her gaze over his all-too-tempting features. God, that body...

She shut her eyes, but it was too late. The image of him was burned into her retinas.

Could she be any more pathetic?

They barely knew each other, and here she was imagining him naked, doing things to her that definitely didn't bear thinking about, especially at the nurses' station on a med-surg floor at St. Mary's.

Besides, Adam was all wrong for her. She'd known it from the start, and the fact that he was technically no longer her responsibility didn't change that.

He was still too young. Too keen on returning to the opposite coast. And he wasn't interested in starting a family.

She opened her eyes and looked up at him. He was still waiting for an answer.

"I have to go," she said, with real regret. Carefully, she set the cup down and logged out from her patient's chart. "I have clinic in a few minutes."

"What about dinner?" he asked.

"Sorry," she shook her head, "but I can't."

CHAPTER 8

Friday morning, Lena woke up to a ringing phone and the news that her mother was back in the ER.

"What happened?" she asked Cristina, the woman she'd hired to look after her mom.

"*Senora* Nina, she no listen," Cristina said. "Every day, same thing. I tell her, no stairs. Use commode. She argue, say she don't need commode. Today, she try going up the stairs and fall down. The ambulance come, take her to hospital."

Lena slid out of bed and headed for the shower. "I'll be there as soon as I can. Can you stay at the house until I call you?"

"*Si,*" the woman said. "But your *madre*, she stubborn. How I can take care of her if she no listen?"

Thankfully this was Lena's Friday off. She still had a couple post-op patients to round on and discharge from the hospital this morning. But after that, she'd drive down to Cedars to take care of the latest crisis.

Several hours later, while waiting for her mother's orthopedist to review the X-rays, Lena called her sister. "Mom fell. I'm in the ER with her."

Zhanna's sigh grated on Lena's already-frayed nerves. "I told you she'd be better off in a nursing home."

"That's not an option," Lena said.

"What's the alternative?"

A nurse entered with some pain medication.

"I'll be right back, Ma," Lena said, ducking out of the curtain-enclosed cubicle. Down the hall, she found an unoccupied corner next to a clean linen cart. "You don't have stairs, Zhanna."

"Oh, no," her sister said. "No way. You are not saddling me with Mom."

"It's just for a week or so."

"Patrick won't like it," Zhanna said.

"She's your mother. I'm sure if you explain the situation, he'll agree."

"I can't," Zhanna said. "He's under a lot of stress with work."

"So am I," Lena retorted. "Look, Mom just needs a place to stay. I'm not talking about helping her with the everyday stuff. She has a caregiver for that—"

"Why don't *you* take her?"

Lena gritted her teeth. "I don't have a spare bedroom."

"You've got a study, don't you? Put a hospital bed in there. And you're a doctor. If anything happens, you'll know what to do."

"I'm hardly ever home."

"So?" Zhanna said. "You hired a caregiver, a trained professional, right? Let *her* deal with Mom."

Lena sighed and leaned back against the wall. What had she expected? Zhanna was just being herself. She always had some ready excuse for why she couldn't help out, or why she had to bail at the last minute on the rare occasion when she did agree to help. The kids had ballet or a playdate or something else that required Zhanna to drive or supervise, or both. And if it wasn't the kids, it was Patrick. Zhanna needed to pick up his dry cleaning, or iron his shirts, or have dinner on the table the moment he got home. Sometimes Lena wanted to snap, *Let Patrick get his own damn dinner.* Surely the man could manage once in a while without Zhanna around.

Then again, what did Lena know? As her sister frequently pointed out, she wasn't married and didn't have children. What she had was a career that gave her financial independence and the ability to control her own schedule. Or so Zhanna claimed.

Rather than get into another argument, Lena ended the call.

Just in time, too. A lanky, dark-haired man in scrubs entered her mother's cubicle. Lena hurried to join them.

"You need to slow down," the man was telling her mother.

"I'll slow down when I'm in the grave," Lena's mother said, glancing up as Lena approached the bed. "Ah, here she is. My daughter, Lena. This is Dr. Cohen, who did my hip."

"Gabe Cohen." He offered her a warm handshake. "We spoke on the phone. I was just telling your mother that her X-rays look good. No new fracture, and the prosthesis is well-positioned. She can go home."

"What about weight-bearing?" Lena asked.

"As tolerated," Dr. Cohen said, before turning to address her mother. "But let's agree, Mrs. Shapiro, no stairs until the physical therapist says you're ready."

It took another several hours to make all the arrangements.

A call to Rachel to update her on the latest developments netted the unexpected bonus of assistance from Erik's college-aged sons, who were spending the summer with Erik and Rachel.

They made short work of disassembling and transporting the rented hospital bed from Nina Shapiro's house to Lena's condo. Under Lena's supervision, they cleared out and rearranged her study, pushing aside or removing office furniture and electronics to make room for her mother's things.

The local medical supply store provided a treasure trove of safety accessories that allowed Lena to transform the guest bathroom for her mother's use. She quickly set up the raised toilet seat with built-in arms, a shower chair, and no-slip rubber mats. With a few tips gleaned from YouTube videos, she even managed to install strategically-located grab bars.

While the caregiver helped Nina settle in to her new

quarters, Lena did a final sweep through the living/dining area, checking for any tripping hazards.

Then she ordered dinner from the café down the street, and headed to the bathroom to wash away the dirt and stress of the day.

~

Lena wasn't sure how she ended up spending most of Sunday making poppy seed strudel with her mother.

It was a ritual from her childhood, something she and her mother used to do for birthdays and holidays, back when Lena's father was still alive. They'd crack open the windows in the sweltering kitchen and, while Zhanna played with dolls at their feet, they would spend hours mixing the ingredients, kneading the dough and waiting for it to rise. It was Lena's job to punch it down and flatten it before they divided it up and rolled each dough ball out into a ten-inch square, then spread the poppy seed filling on top. Side by side, they'd roll the sheets into thick logs, which they'd transfer to greased baking sheets.

"I called the home health agency," Lena said as they waited for the filled dough to rise again. "They weren't sure if they had a physical therapist who could come out here tomorrow."

Nina whisked the remaining egg yolk in a small bowl. "I know what exercises to do."

"That's good. But it helps to have a professional who can monitor your progress and show you new exercises when you're ready." Lena turned on the oven to preheat. "If the agency doesn't call back, you need to call them again tomorrow. Unless you want me to do that?"

Nina dismissed the offer with a wave of her flour-dusted hand. "I can manage."

"You won't forget?"

"There's nothing wrong with my memory." She brushed the tops of each roll with egg yolk. "You'll take one of these for your friend Erik's boys. Thank them for their help."

"I'm sure they'll appreciate it."

"I'll save one for Dr. Cohen, too," Nina said. "I see him Wednesday. We'll need to leave by ten in the morning to be there on time."

Lena glanced up. "Cristina will drive you."

"You're not coming?" Nina frowned.

"I have office hours, Ma."

"You work too much."

"You did too." Lena picked specks of dried dough off the table. "Especially after Dad died."

All those people bringing shoe boxes stuffed with jumbled receipts. Lena remembered waking up at night and seeing her mother still at the kitchen table, sorting receipts and filling out tax forms.

Nina pursed her lips. "I had no choice then. Two children to feed, and no husband…"

"I know, Ma. And I appreciate that you didn't let us starve."

"You think this is a joke?"

Lena dropped her eyes. "No, of course not."

Nina humphed and wiped her hands on a tea towel. "You and your sister have options that I didn't have."

"I know."

"Zhanna I'm not so worried about. She's settled. But you…I want you to have a good life. What good is a fancy degree and high-paying job if you're alone?"

Lena sighed. *Not this again.*

"You're thirty-nine years old, Lena." She slid the first tray of rolls into the oven. "You know Masha's youngest just got married and is already expecting a baby? This will be her fifth grandchild."

"Good for her."

Her mother shot her a reproving look. "You should show more respect."

"I show plenty of respect, Ma."

"At least your sister understands the importance of family. If not for her, I'd still be waiting for grandchildren."

Lena gritted her teeth. *Where was your precious Zhanna when you were in the hospital, Ma?* she wanted to say. *And what about now? Which daughter turned her life upside down so you could avoid that nursing home you claim to hate so much?*

But she swallowed the words, because what was the point? Her mother saw what she wanted to see. And two grandchildren made up for a multitude of sins.

CHAPTER 9

Adam pushed open the door with his free hand and entered the doctors' lounge, quickly scanning the room.

There she was. Finally.

He strode past the refreshments table and the silent bank of computers, bypassed multiple unoccupied sofas and armchairs, and took a seat across from Lena. She'd kicked off her rubber clogs and burrowed into the corner of an overstuffed armchair, one leg tucked beneath her, the other dangling over the side.

Whatever she was reading on her phone must have been riveting, because she didn't even look up, though he made no effort to be quiet.

He took another bite of poppy-filled roll and pondered his approach.

"You should try this," he said after another few beats of silence. "It's amazing."

"Hm?" She glanced up and blinked, eyes focusing on his lips and then belatedly on the half-demolished piece of strudel he was holding.

He smiled and lifted the napkin with a second slice toward her. "I grabbed two before they all disappeared, but I'm willing to share."

"No, thanks." She sat up straight and slipped the clogs back on. "I brought it in for the OR staff. My mother and I baked this weekend."

"Wow. My compliments to you and your mother." He contemplated the swirl of poppy seeds, nuts, and raisins surrounded by sweet dough. "You think it's possible to get high from this?"

Her lips quirked. "No. But it might show up on a urine tox screen."

"No kidding." He finished off the second slice in three bites and wiped his fingers on the napkin. "I'll take my chances. So, is your mom doing better?"

Lena's eyes drifted back to her phone. "Getting there."

"What are you reading?"

She sighed and turned off the phone before he could lean over to look.

"Nothing," she said, slipping the device into the breast pocket of her scrubs. "How are things going with Erik?"

"Great. We just ran a case list for the week, and there's plenty of pathology to keep me busy."

She nodded and stood up. "That's good."

"You're running away again," Adam said, slowly rising to his feet.

She swallowed, then turned to check the wall clock. "I have a case at three."

"Which means you can spare me five minutes."

"Adam..." She paused, flicked a glance around the empty lounge. Looking for what? Inspiration? Distraction? Rescue in the form of a third party? Apparently finding none of the above, she sighed again and focused her gaze over his shoulder. "I'm sorry if you feel I'm giving you the runaround—"

"Are you?"

Her lips tightened. "I'm sure you're a great guy. But this isn't going to work."

"Why not?" He stepped closer. Beneath the smell of hospital disinfectant, he caught the faint whiff of something flowery, exotic. She still wore the surgical cap from her last case, and he wanted to rip it off, bury his nose in her hair. "We had fun that night, didn't we?"

He could see the pulse flickering at the base of her throat. His own heart rate accelerated. If not for the fact that they both had to be in the OR soon, he'd have closed the space between them and done what he'd been dreaming of doing for days. He could almost feel her skin beneath his fingers, the soft lips parting for him as he leaned down to taste her.

She stepped back. "I'm thirty-nine."

Her tone—sharp and defensive—pierced through his erotic thoughts. And then the words registered and he blinked.

She raised her chin, as if bracing for his response.

"Would you believe," he said, biting back a smile, "I have a thing for older women?"

~

Later that night, over a solitary dinner of moo shu pork eaten straight from the container, Adam admitted to himself that as far as pickup lines went, that one hadn't gone over too well. Even though the sentiment behind it was true.

Hell, most of his past relationships were with older women, starting with Mary Lou Denton in junior high. Mary Lou was nine months older than him and half a foot taller when they were paired in PE for the dance unit. For an entire month, he'd box-stepped in a lust-filled fog, imagining what it would be like to slide his sweaty palm from her waist all the way up to her budding breasts. Years later, when they bumped into each other at a mutual friend's wedding, he'd laughingly confessed his schoolboy crush, and before the night was over, she'd invited him do much more than his seventh-grade self had ever dared imagine.

Maybe it went back to the fact that he'd grown up surrounded by women. Nannies, housekeepers, an entire array of domestic staff, almost exclusively female. And then there were his sisters, both older, and a gaggle of female cousins. If he kept quiet and out of the way, they let him tag along. Or maybe they simply forgot about him. Which was just as well, because he learned more about life from their unfiltered conversations than he did from all his years of formal education at the private prep school and Ivy League university he attended.

The tutelage continued well into his twenties. Whenever he took a breather from studying and working, he enjoyed being the stand-in plus-one for his sisters' and cousins' friends. In exchange for the favor, his dates offered him the benefit of their experience, both in and out of bed.

He learned to appreciate the qualities that came with maturity. A woman who valued her independence and felt secure enough in her own skin to not need the constant reassurance of a man—*that* fired up his libido, even more than a woman's physical beauty.

When he'd decided to pursue Lena, her age hadn't been a consideration. The attraction had been immediate, visceral. But the more he saw her in action, the more he realized that she embodied all the things he admired most. Intelligence, strength, grace. And what she apparently saw as a drawback— her age—*he* felt enhanced her desirability.

Too bad she turned it around, making it sound as if *he* had some sort of unnatural fetish that she refused to indulge.

What was eight years' difference anyway? People wouldn't think twice if he'd been the one who was older. But good luck convincing Lena of that.

"Maybe it's the ticking biological clock," his sister Amanda said later that week, over the phone. She'd managed to extract the story from him in between helping her oldest with homework and negotiating a cease-fire between the other two.

"Sorry," she said, with a breathless laugh after yet another interruption from her kids. "Must be a full moon or something."

"Or something," he said, propping his feet up on the living room coffee table. "I'm not sure I buy that ticking clock thing. Just because you're pregnant again doesn't mean every woman has babies on the brain."

"Maybe not, but—oh, geez, not again." She broke off, and Adam grinned at the sounds of entropy in action, three thousand miles away. A dull thud, then Amanda's raised voice: "Matthew, Jacob, that's enough! I'm telling you for the last time—one more word out of either one of you, and the electronics go away for a *month*!"

"Wow," Adam said when she was back on the line. "You're scary when you're mad."

"Better believe it," Amanda said. "Where were we?"

"Discussing my love life."

"Or lack thereof," she quipped.

Adam slumped down further on the couch. "Go ahead, rub it in. Come Christmas, Matthew and Jacob are getting a drum set. Each."

"You wouldn't!"

"Help me out here, Mandy. I need some insight into the female psyche."

"I don't know," Amanda said. "Maybe she doesn't like men."

Adam snorted. In his mind's eye he could still see Lena's expression at that moment just before she detonated the age bomb. Hungry. Like she'd just come off a ketogenic diet and he was a slice of death-by-chocolate cake.

He swallowed and shifted on the couch. "I think we can rule that out."

"Well, then, you must be losing your touch, baby bro. When was the last time a woman turned you down? Not counting this one."

He scratched his chin, the itchy bristles reminding him he hadn't shaved for the third day in a row. Any longer, and some administrator might cite him for violating OSHA standards.

"Hey," Amanda said. "It's not the end of the world. Tell you what...remember my friend Zoe, from Vassar? Some studio optioned her book and she's in L.A. now, working on the script. I have her number here. Somewhere. I'll text it to you and you can give her a call."

Now he saw that the downside of having been so agreeable

over the years was that the setup offers kept rolling in, long after he was no longer interested in playing the game.

"Thanks, Mandy, but I don't need a pity date."

"This isn't a pity date," she said. "Zoe's great fun, you'll like her. And you're both at loose ends, in a strange city, so it's a win-win."

Perseverance was clearly a family trait, because twenty minutes after hanging up, Amanda texted him a phone number, along with instructions.

CALL HER, the message read. All caps.

Adam shook his head and went back to lacing up his sneakers.

His second choice for working off sexual frustration was to hit the weight room. Good thing his gym was open late.

CHAPTER 10

Lena was in the office, about to see her fourth patient of the morning when her mother's caregiver called.

"Your *madre*, she lock herself in the bathroom and refuse to come out."

Lena closed her eyes and leaned against the wall just outside the exam room. "Did she say why?"

"She say she don't need my help."

Great. All Lena needed was for her mother to have another slip and fall that would land her back in the ER.

"Can you please put her on the phone?" Lena said.

A muffled exchange of words ensued, and then Cristina returned. "She say she will call you later."

Later turned out to be mid-afternoon. Lena wrapped up her post-op visit with a patient who was two weeks out from thyroid surgery, then took the call from her office.

"What's going on, Ma?" she asked.

"That woman," Nina Shapiro said. "*Kakaya zanuda!* She won't leave me in peace. Don't do this, don't do that. I am not a child. I know what I can and cannot do without her constantly telling me. I can bathe without her breathing down my neck."

"I'm sure she's just trying to help," Lena said.

"She can help by doing what I ask," Nina said. "Or she can stay out of my way."

Lena counted to ten. "Ma, I know you like being independent. You'll get there, I promise. But you need to give it time, okay? Pushing too hard too fast is what gets people in trouble."

"Sitting around doing nothing is what gets people in trouble," Nina grumbled. "I need to go to the store, but Cristina won't take me. I told her I'll give her money so she can go herself. But no, she won't do that either unless she checks with you first, because you hired her. So I said my daughter might have hired you, but *I* can still fire you—"

Lena groaned. "You didn't, did you? She's still there?"

"For now," Nina said. "But if she doesn't start listening to me and being reasonable…"

Lena rolled her eyes. *Pot, meet kettle.* "I did a huge shop over the weekend, Ma. There should still be plenty of food in the fridge. Have Cristina make you something for dinner. Or order in. There's a stack of takeout menus in the kitchen drawer, next to the dishwasher."

"Takeout?" Nina said. "What person in their right mind would eat takeout when they could have homemade *borscht* and *kotleti* instead? All I need is a few ingredients."

"You can cook some other time," Lena gritted out. "Let Cristina do it for now. You should be resting, or doing the exercises the physical therapist showed you."

"You don't understand," Nina said. "Masha is coming to dinner tomorrow—"

"*What?* Since when?"

Nina's tone turned defensive. "She called to see how I was doing. I told her that I was tired of sitting here all day, staring at four walls. So tomorrow night she's coming for dinner. She said she'll bring her *salyonie agurtsiy* and *kvashenaya kapusta*. You cannot expect me to serve her takeout. I need beets and fresh chicken and *grechka*—and not that ground-up garbage they sell in boxes."

Lena rubbed her forehead, already dreading the weekend.

Her mother would no doubt rope her into helping with the meal prep, then insist that she join them for dinner. She'd get double the usual dose of intrusive personal questions, and would be forced to listen with polite interest as her mother and Masha dissected the lives of relatives and friends, most of whom Lena had never met.

Still, it was easier to give in than to argue. "Fine, Ma. Cristina will buy what you need. *If* you promise to sit and relax and not do anything the therapist said you're not ready to do."

"Good, good," Nina said. "She can go to *Odessa*."

"Trader Joe's is much closer—"

"Trader Joe's won't have what I need. I'll get the list. You talk to Cristina." And then she was gone.

Lena sighed, foiled by the same stubbornness and persistence that had enabled her mother to raise two girls on her own while supporting the family by doing other peoples' taxes.

Her mother was probably right about Trader Joe's. It was great for Lena's everyday needs, and she couldn't imagine what she'd do without their selection of ready-to-eat salads and frozen meals. But for what sounded like a traditional full-course dinner, the Russian market in West Hollywood was a better bet.

As a kid, Lena would troop down the street to *Odessa* every week, first with her mother, and then on her own, armed with a grocery list and an earful of instructions. *Keep an eye on the scale when they're weighing out kielbasa. Check the eyes and gills to make sure the herring is fresh. Don't get distracted by the halvah and imported candy.*

If she closed her eyes, she could still smell the pickles and fish and feel the blast of cold air from the freezer filled with bags of *pelmeni*.

The medical assistant tapped on Lena's door. "Patient in room one."

Lena nodded. "Be there in a minute."

When Cristina answered, she sounded relieved. Because of Lena's reassurance that her job was secure? Or because she looked forward to several hours away from Nina Shapiro's company?

"*Sí, Doctora*," she told Lena. "If you say is okay, I drive. No problem."

She was more than happy to search for whatever exotic ingredients Nina Shapiro needed, even if it meant braving L.A. traffic all the way to West Hollywood and back.

~

"So what's the verdict?" Rachel asked that evening, when Lena rejoined her at the nurses' station in the ER. "Surgery or antibiotics?"

"Both." Lena logged into the computer to do a quick consult note. She wasn't on call, but she'd still been in the office finishing up charts when Rachel called about a patient with acute abdominal pain.

"He got his first Zosyn dose an hour ago," Rachel said, watching Lena type. "His pain's controlled, and we're tanking him up with IV fluids. He's NPO just in case."

Lena nodded without looking up. "Bowel rest wouldn't hurt. Poor guy. Third bout of diverticulitis in six months. He needs a sigmoidectomy, but I'd prefer to do it electively once he's cooled down with the antibiotics. Which hospitalist is on tonight?"

Rachel checked the roster tacked up behind the counter and reached for the phone. "Wolf Knox."

Lena listened with half an ear as Rachel gave Wolf a thirty-second summary of the patient's history, presentation, and treatment to date.

Wolf must have responded with his usual irreverent humor, because Rachel laughed and said, "Is it live? No? Oh, okay, but you'll let me know? Great, see you in a few."

"What was that about?" Lena asked after Rachel ended the call.

"He started humming the colonoscopy song." At Lena's blank look, Rachel said, "He and Doug did an impromptu version of it at the 4th of July barbecue, remember?"

Lena shrugged. "I had to leave early."

"Oh, that's right. Too bad. I almost peed myself halfway through. Wolf's uploading the video to YouTube. You have to see it. He promised to send me the link. I'll forward it to you."

Lena logged off the computer. "I should get going. When does your shift end?"

Rachel glanced at the time. "Half an hour ago. I just need to sign out my patients. Want to grab a quick bite?"

"I thought you and Erik had plans."

"He called," Rachel said. "His last case ran over, so...You know how it is."

Too well.

Lena hesitated, then nodded. "Let me call Cristina and see if she's back and can stay a bit longer."

An hour later, they were weaving their way through the crowd at O'Brien's toward an unoccupied booth in the back. Lena nodded and smiled at a few familiar faces as they passed. Thanks to its proximity to St. Mary's, the pub was a favorite among hospital staff.

"Don't look now," Rachel said, "but Dr. McHottie's over there by the pool table."

Lena glanced around, but her view was blocked by a rowdy group of college kids making their way toward the bar. "Dr. McHottie?"

"Adam Sterling," Rachel said. "That's what the nurses are calling him. You've got to admit, the guy is smokin'."

Lena stumbled slightly before righting herself. "Does Erik know you talk like that when he's not around?"

Rachel laughed. "Come on, Lena, lighten up. I may be married and pregnant, but I'm not blind."

Lena waited until after they were seated and had placed their orders before letting her gaze wander. And yes, there he was. Tall, casually dressed in a T-shirt and jeans, and definitely smokin' hot.

And he wasn't alone. A woman with spiky red hair and multiple piercings was plastered against his side, a proprietary hand curled around his bicep. He grinned at something she said and offered her his cue stick. She accepted with a laugh, then sauntered around the pool table and leaned forward to line up her shot, giving Adam and whoever else might be watching an unobstructed view of her cleavage.

"Hey." Rachel waved a hand in front of Lena. "You okay?"

Lena forced herself to look away. "Fine."

"You sure?" Rachel cocked her head. "For a minute there, you looked like you wanted to throw up."

"I'm fine," Lena repeated.

So what if Adam hooked up with the redhead? He could hook up with as many women as he wanted. Lena didn't care. She'd turned him down, and what he chose to do after that was his business. Lena had her own agenda, and that didn't include Adam.

A harried server deposited their drinks and burgers before rushing off to another table. For several minutes, they ate without talking, the noise of a dozen competing conversations flowing around them.

"I signed up with a sperm bank," Lena said abruptly.

Rachel choked on a fry and started coughing. "You *what?*" she finally managed, after downing half a glass of water.

"I signed up with a sperm bank," Lena repeated. "Figured I couldn't afford to wait any longer."

"But...a *sperm bank?*"

"I want a child, Rach. There aren't too many options. It's either assisted reproduction or adoption, and frankly my odds are way better with assisted reproduction."

"But...on your own?"

"Lots of women choose to go it alone," Lena said. "It's a thing now. Single moms by choice. There's a ton of online resources and support groups. Practically an entire industry to help navigate the process."

Rachel studied her. "You're serious about this."

"I know it's not going to be easy," Lena said. "My mom will probably disown me. But I was hoping I could at least count on my best friend to support my decision..."

Rachel reached across the table and clasped her hand. "I'm

sorry, Lena. Of course you can count on me."

"Just think—if this works, our kids will grow up together. Wouldn't that be amazing?"

"Amazing," Rachel echoed. Then, apparently sensing Lena's disappointment at her response, she added with forced enthusiasm, "So what's the plan? Do you have a donor?"

"Not yet. I've been looking through the online catalog. You wouldn't believe the selection. Whatever you want in terms of ethnicity, religion, hair and eye color, body build, IQ." Lena paused and glanced again toward the pool table.

Adam was no longer there. Neither was his companion. Lena clenched her jaw and scanned the crowd, but couldn't find them anywhere. *Stop it,* she told herself sternly. *What he does is none of your business.*

"What happens once you pick someone?" Rachel asked.

Lena jerked her attention back to the conversation. "I visit my OB, get a prescription for Clomid, and order a few vials. Assuming there are no issues, I can probably do an IUI sometime next month."

"Wow," Rachel said. "You're not wasting any time, are you?"

Lena folded her napkin and ran a finger along the crease. Some people might argue that at her age, intrauterine insemination itself was a waste of time, and she'd have a greater chance of success by going straight to in-vitro fertilization. But that was a much more invasive procedure, not to mention way more expensive. If she was planning on being a single parent, especially here in L.A., where the cost of living was among the highest in the country, she'd better learn to conserve her resources.

"If IUI doesn't work," she said, "I'll still need to do IVF. And you know how long that can take. So..." She trailed off and shrugged.

Rachel reached over and squeezed her hand again. "Don't worry," she said. "You'll do fine. And if you want someone to go with you, just let me know. I'm an old hand at this stuff."

CHAPTER 11

For the second weekend in a row, Lena was reminded of how time- and labor-intensive cooking from scratch could be.

She usually ate on the run, relying on grab-and-go meals from the hospital cafeteria or Trader Joe's, supplemented with takeout and the occasional dinner out.

But Saturday, she spent hours in the kitchen with her mother. Peeling, then boiling beets, carrots and potatoes. Chopping onion and pickles and smoked ham. Prepping chicken for the meat grinder that her mother insisted she needed from home.

"And while you're there," Nina said, "you can get my gray dress with the flowers. It's hanging in my closet upstairs."

By the time Lena returned, the familiar scent of frying onion permeated the condo, and suddenly she was ten again, sitting at the kitchen table with her mother while Zhanna napped upstairs, digging into a bowl of *grechnevaya kasha*, the sweet taste of caramelized onion cooked in butter melting in her mouth.

Strange to think that Lena was older now than her mother had been then.

Nina glanced up from the cutting board, where she was using a sharp paring knife to peel the slightly charred skin off a baked eggplant.

"Good, you're back." She shifted on the cushioned chair she'd been using on and off through the day and nodded at the box Lena was holding. "You can set that up on the counter. I'll need your help making *farsh*."

Lena followed her mother's instructions, grinding the raw chicken she'd prepped earlier. Her mother added chopped onion, eggs, bread soaked in milk, and seasoning, and together they shaped each spoonful of *farsh* into flattened oval patties for frying.

Nina washed her hands at the kitchen sink while Lena manned the stove.

"How's your hip?" Lena asked a short while later.

"Fine." Nina slowly turned the metal-frame front-wheeled walker and headed for the hall. "I'll be back in five minutes. Don't let the *kotleti* burn."

Lena watched her mother's laborious progress, poised to spring forward at the first sign of trouble. She'd made the mistake of offering her help earlier, and gotten snapped at for her efforts. Now she just gritted her teeth and stood back, watching and waiting.

"Do you want some ibuprofen?" she asked when her mother returned from the restroom.

"Not yet." Nina checked the clock. "I'll take it with dinner. You should go take a shower and get dressed. Our guests will be here in an hour."

"Guests, as in plural?" Lena frowned. "I thought it was just Masha."

Nina raised her brows, innocence incarnate. "Didn't I mention? Her nephew is visiting from Seattle. So of course I told her to bring him along."

Lena should have guessed something was up from the quantity of food her mother insisted on preparing. *Leftovers for tomorrow*, Nina said. *Borscht always tastes better on the second day.* And Lena was foolish enough to accept that at face value.

Not anymore. "How old is this nephew?" she asked.

Nina busied herself at the table, chopping fresh dill for

garnish. "Forty-two…"

Ugh, not again. She'd been set up. No wonder her mother had been so cagey. What Lena needed was an excuse to escape. Maybe she'd set her phone to ring during the soup course. A hospital emergency, she'd tell her mother.

"…divorced last year," Nina continued, "but Masha says the wife was terrible. *Nastoyaschaya sterva.* Sasha is lucky to be rid of her."

Lena flicked off the burner and transferred the last batch of *kotleti* to a warming dish. "I can't believe you'd do this to me."

"What?" Nina said, slapping the knife down on the table. "He's smart. A biomedical engineer from the University of Washington, here to give a talk at UCLA."

"I don't care if he's the fucking head of the United Nations—"

"You watch your mouth," Nina said. "And show some respect. You could do a lot worse than a university professor."

Lena clenched her jaw. "You're missing the point."

"And this point would be?"

"You went behind my back. You and Masha conspired to set me up. After I specifically told you not to."

Nina waved the objection away. "You said that when we were talking about Dr. Cohen. And I did not set you up with him."

"Oh, please," Lena said. "I'm sure you would have tried. Thank goodness for that photo on his desk of him and his wife and kids. It saved us all some embarrassment—"

"I don't know why Cristina had to mention that to you," Nina sniffed. "A mother wants her children to be happy. You will understand that, when you have your own children."

"I don't want or need you to be playing matchmaker."

"Well, if you showed any interest in meeting a nice man yourself and settling down, then I wouldn't need to—"

"Stop," Lena said. "Just—stop."

They stared at each other for a moment, then Lena shook her head and stalked out of the kitchen.

Her mother's voice followed her. "Someday you'll thank

me, Lena. When you have a husband and children, you'll remember today and say thank you for making this happen. You'll see."

~

"Oh, hey," Adam said, looking up from the Keurig machine in the doctors' lounge. "What are you doing here?"

Lena sank into a nearby armchair and closed her eyes. "Don't ask."

The coffee machine hissed. Adam removed his cup of Dark Roast and tossed out the used pod. "Want some coffee?"

"No, thanks. It's too late for caffeine."

"Not for me. I'm on call." He took a seat. "By the way, Mrs. Patel got admitted with a PE—"

"What?" Lena's eyes flew open. A pulmonary embolus, or PE, was every surgeon's nightmare. Cancer patients like Mrs. Patel, whose sigmoid colon she and Adam had resected several weeks ago, were at particular risk for developing post-operative clots.

"I happened to be in the ER doing a consult, so I saw her," Adam said. "Unofficially, since this time it's not a surgical case. But she was happy to see a familiar face."

"Who admitted her?" Lena asked.

"Wolf Knox. She's on Xarelto now, getting some IV fluids and oxygen. If she does well overnight, she'll probably go home tomorrow."

Lena nodded and let out a sigh. "I should swing by and see her."

"I'll go with you."

"No need." Lena headed for the bank of computers along the wall, where she logged in to check the patient's chart.

Adam finished his coffee and tossed the cup, then joined Lena on her way to the med-surg floor where Mrs. Patel's room was located.

"Don't you have something else to do?" Lena said.

He smiled and shrugged. "Not really. It's been pretty quiet, other than that one consult."

"So go home."

He cocked his head. "Dr. Shapiro, are you trying to get rid of me?"

"It doesn't seem to be working," she said, stopping at the elevators. She jabbed the *Up* button, then glanced at him and frowned at his frank appraisal. "What?"

"Just admiring your ensemble."

She glanced down at the teal silk dress her mother had insisted she wear. Beneath it, her legs were bare, and her feet were shoved into a spare pair of running shoes that she always kept in her trunk. "I was in a rush," she said. "And I wasn't planning to spend my evening here."

The elevator pinged, and he followed her inside. "How *were* you planning to spend your evening?"

She shrugged, and he let the issue go until after they finished seeing Mrs. Patel.

"Where to now?" he asked, when she remained silent on the ride down to the lobby.

She hesitated and checked her watch. "I'm going to watch some CNN."

He kept pace with her, all the way back to the doctors' lounge. When he moved to follow her inside, she turned to face him, blocking his way, her arms folded across her chest. "I thought you were going home."

He studied her for a moment before saying softly, "I'm not in any rush. And I'm a good listener."

She swallowed and shook her head, then dropped her arms and swiveled to stalk into the lounge. Swiping the remote control from a cabinet beneath the large-screen TV, she settled onto a sofa and turned on the news. She didn't react when Adam joined her on the sofa, sprawling out beside her. Not quite touching, but near enough that she could feel the heat of his big body, and hear his breath beneath the drone of the news anchor.

The minutes ticked by.

Her stomach growled, reminding her that she'd skipped out

on the dinner she and her mother had so laboriously prepared. Would there be anything left over when she returned in a few hours? Or would her mother, out of spite, pack everything up in plastic containers for Masha and her nephew to take home?

Adam shifted. "I have some steaks in the fridge, if you're interested."

"Thanks," she said. "But I'm okay."

"Two steaks are as easy to throw on the grill as one." He paused. "And I think I have CNN too."

Her lips curved in a faint smile. "You think?"

"Probably," he said. "I prefer ESPN, but the cable company throws in some other channels for free."

Her stomach rumbled again, deciding the issue. "Do you have any wine or beer to go with that steak?"

He chuckled. "I'm sure I could scrounge up something."

She accepted his hand up. He released her as soon as she was on her feet, and her relief was tinged with a hint of disappointment.

Strange. She'd been so eager to escape grabby Sasha earlier that evening that she'd rushed out without her phone and wallet, and it wasn't until after she got to her car that she realized she was barefoot.

Adam might be pushy and unbelievably persistent—he'd have to be, considering the number of times she'd rebuffed him, and yet here they were, driving to his house. But she had to admit, his touch left her...breathless.

Quite a contrast to the crawling skin sensation she'd experienced with Masha's nephew, who'd taken the seating arrangement at dinner as an invitation to grope Lena beneath the tablecloth while her mother and his aunt chatted just a few feet away. She'd edged her chair away, but he failed to take the hint, and merely squeezed her thigh harder when she hissed "Stop it!" beneath her breath. When her phone finally rang, she'd jumped up from the table to answer it, then muttered something about having to see a patient at the hospital, and grabbed her keys on her way out the door.

"Here we are," Adam said, ushering her into a Spanish-style

bungalow and flicking on the lights.

He toed off his shoes near the entryway, and Lena followed suit. Rugs with bold geometric designs covered the floor, and large abstract prints lined the walls.

"Nice," Lena said, as she followed Adam down the hall toward the back of the house.

"It came furnished, so I can't take any credit. Living room's that way. Bathroom, study, kitchen—" he pointed out each room as they passed. "Make yourself at home."

Instead of planting herself in front of the wall-mounted screen in the living room, Lena trailed Adam into the kitchen. Sliding glass doors led out to a small patio, where Adam fired up a gas barbecue and lit several citronella candles that stood in the center of a wrought iron table.

Lena stepped out and glanced around. A profusion of pink and purple bougainvillea covered the walls of the small enclosed backyard. Potted succulents competed for space with miniature citrus trees. The soothing burble of water had her crossing the patio, the flagstones beneath her bare feet still warm from the heat of the day. She found the wall-mounted fountain half-hidden beneath flowering vines. For several minutes she just stood there, her hand cupped beneath the cool water flowing from the mouth of a stone gargoyle.

"We can eat out here, if you like," Adam said.

She turned to find him standing a short distance behind her, holding a bottle of Cabernet Sauvignon.

"I'd like," she said.

He nodded and lifted the bottle. "Red okay with you?"

"Sure."

She watched him peel the foil and uncork the wine, his movements as elegant and efficient as they were in the OR. He poured a glass and offered it to her.

"You're not having any?" she said, when she noticed he'd brought only one glass.

"I'm on call through the weekend," he said, reaching for a bottle of mineral water that he'd deposited on the table earlier.

Over a dinner of steaks and salad, which he whipped up

with remarkable speed, Lena relaxed enough to unload the whole sorry story of her mother's botched matchmaking attempt.

"She thinks a woman isn't complete without a man," Lena said. "Even though *she* spent the last sixteen years without one."

Adam topped up her glass. "What happened to your dad?"

"He died when I was thirteen. Brain aneurysm."

"I'm sorry," he said. "And your mother never remarried?"

"No." She took another sip of wine and sighed. "Maybe if I move to the other side of the world, she'll stop meddling."

He smiled. "Where would you go?"

"I don't know." She absently stroked the stem of her wineglass. "Australia, maybe. Or New Zealand. Somewhere where they speak English and I could still practice medicine."

"Wouldn't it be easier—and less disruptive—to just tell your mom to back off?"

Lena laughed. "Oh, sure. Like I've haven't told her *that* a thousand times. Does your mom listen when you tell her to butt out?"

He cocked his head and seemed to give it some thought. "I'm not sure I ever told her that."

"Really?"

"You have to understand my parents," he said. "They don't get involved in the day-to-day stuff. That's for staff to deal with. You know, nannies, housekeepers, personal assistants. It saves a lot of aggravation."

"Wow. That sounds so..." Lena trailed off, searching for the right word. Cold. Lonely. Miserable.

Angry as she was with her mother, at least Lena knew she cared enough to get involved.

She pushed the thought aside and focused on Adam. "Was there anything your parents *didn't* delegate?"

"Oh, sure." He reached for the wine bottle and topped up her glass. "My dad liked to talk about *Important Things*. Still does."

"What does he consider important?"

"The family name. The family business." He grinned ruefully. "I can't tell you how many lectures we had to sit through as kids about the duty we had to honor Grandpa Sterling's memory and carry on his legacy. For God and country. Not to mention the Sterling family coffers."

Lena spluttered out a laugh. "What does your family do? Manufacture weapons?"

"Not quite," he said. "Though legend has it my grandfather started the business during World War II, when the government was recruiting civilian companies to produce penicillin for the army. There's a plaque in my dad's office commemorating Grandpa Sterling's contribution to the war effort."

"Wow," Lena said. "That *is* impressive."

"Yeah, well the story loses its luster after you've heard it a few hundred times." He scraped back his chair and rose. "But enough about me. You want some dessert? I have ice cream."

"No, thanks. I should get going." Lena got up. "This was lovely, thank you."

"Coffee, then." He preempted her refusal by adding, "I've got decaf."

She smiled. "In that case, sure."

They moved between the patio and kitchen, clearing the table, washing and putting away the dishes, their movements so synchronized it was as if they'd done the same routine together a thousand times.

Back at the table, Adam shifted his chair closer before sitting down. Their knees brushed. Lena glanced at him, but didn't move away.

As they sipped coffee, Adam returned to their original topic of conversation.

"So what happens when you're dating?" he asked. "Does your mom back off then?"

"Depends."

"On what?"

"If she sees the guy I'm dating as good son-in-law material."

"Oh, no," he laughed. "There are criteria?"

"You bet." Lena reeled them off on her fingers. "He needs to come from a good family and treat his parents well. Some kind of graduate degree is a must—doctor, lawyer, university professor. Oh, and he has to be Jewish, preferably Ashkenazi. Bonus points if his family's from Russia."

"Well," Adam said, "I guess that eliminates me."

Lena snorted. "That eliminates most men."

"So does she really give you a hard time if you're seeing someone who doesn't pass her son-in-law litmus test?"

"She used to," Lena said. "Which is why I haven't brought anyone home to meet her in years. Not worth the aggravation. Although..."

"What?"

She eyed him, lips pursed. "Now that I'm almost forty, she's getting desperate. Maybe if I show up with someone in tow, she'll be so relieved that I'm not alone, she might give me a pass on the rest..."

"So I'm still in the running?" he joked.

She didn't answer immediately. Instead, she just sat there, fingers absently folding her napkin into ever smaller triangles.

"Lena...?"

She jerked, as if coming out of a trance. "I saw you at O'Brien's last night."

He blinked at the abrupt change of topic. "You did? Why didn't you come by and say hello?"

"It looked like you were on a date."

His brow furrowed. "You mean Zoe?"

She shrugged.

"Yeah, well let's just say you're not the only one who's being set up by family."

Lena narrowed her eyes. "You're telling me that you and this Zoe person were set up?"

"Swear to God." He raised a hand. "My parents might be hands-off, but my sister Amanda? Total busybody. She told me she has this friend from college who recently moved to L.A. and doesn't know anyone, so I should call her. And then she turned around and told Zoe, her friend, the same thing about me. So Zoe called, we met, played some pool, had dinner."

"She seemed..." Lena pursed her lips "...friendly."

"Was that a question?"

"No. I mean, it's none of my business—"

"We parted ways on her doorstep," Adam said. "In case you were wondering."

"I wasn't."

He smiled faintly and studied her. Slowly, giving her plenty of opportunity to pull away, he reached over and traced a finger down her cheek.

Lena didn't move. Didn't blink.

He stroked his thumb over her lower lip, back and forth, as if he had all the time in the world. Again and again. Until her lips parted and he leaned closer.

"You're all flushed," he murmured.

Her eyelids drifted shut. "It's the alcohol."

Sweet, like black cherries, with a hint of licorice and pepper. He tasted it on her lips, more intoxicating than the wine itself.

She sighed into his mouth, the sound like a caress, stoking his already-heightened libido.

He speared his fingers through her hair, dislodging the pins that held the entire mass up. Silky strands tumbled over the backs of his hands, and he groaned, cupping her head and holding her still while he plundered her mouth.

"This is a very bad idea," she whispered, when they finally broke for air.

"Is it?" he said, dipping his head for another taste. She was probably right. He was still on call, and the phone he'd kept by his side throughout the meal could ring at any moment. But even knowing that they might be interrupted, he couldn't let go, couldn't force himself to release Lena. Not when he'd dreamed of her like this, her body soft and pliant in his arms.

She pressed a hand to his chest, right over his racing heart.

His breath hitched. "Lena..."

"Yes." Her fingers slid up, along the collar of his shirt, coming to rest on the back of his neck.

He swallowed. "My bedroom..."

"Yes," she repeated.

Yes.

He grabbed his phone, pulled Lena up, and led the way inside.

~

She felt as if she were moving through a dream. Time slowed. Every detail became magnified. The feel of Adam's hand engulfing hers. The shock of cold ceramic tiles beneath her feet as they crossed the kitchen. The faint whir of the ceiling fan in the bedroom.

Adam flipped a switch. Light flooded the room for a moment, casting the dark wood furniture and massive unmade bed into stark relief.

"Sorry," he muttered, adjusting the dimmer and drawing her further into the room.

She swayed and felt herself falling, the backs of her thighs hitting the mattress, her upper body toppling back onto the covers. Adam followed her down, his mouth and hands resuming their exploration.

Lena closed her eyes, reveling in the pleasure of his touch. His fingers outlined the delicate line of her clavicle to her shoulder, her inner arm, the sensitive hollow of her elbow, all the way down to her fingertips, then back, retracing his path, leaving her trembling and breathless and hungry for more.

His lips brushed the corner of her mouth, her jaw, rested for a moment against the fluttering pulse in her neck, and then drifted down.

She lifted her arms to his neck, the back of his head, fingers burrowing in his hair, encouraging him. Sighing, then gasping as his teeth nipped her skin.

His hand covered her breast, thumb circling the nipple until it puckered beneath the layers of silk and lace.

"Beautiful," he whispered, nudging the material aside and baring her to the cool air. His mouth replaced his hand, closing over her breast and sucking hard. Her eyes flew open and she gasped again as the shock went straight to her core.

He raised his head and looked at her. "You don't need this," he said, tugging at the dress and bra.

She helped him slide them off, then lowered the thong herself. He grinned when she kicked it off.

"Your turn," she said.

He unbuttoned his shirt and shrugged it off, revealing the broad chest and hard muscles she'd only imagined. His eyes caught hers as he undid the belt, and she flushed at the feral hunger she saw there. Slowly, deliberately, he removed the rest of his clothing as she watched.

"Wait," he said when she reached for him.

He fished a condom out from the bedside drawer and tore open the wrapper.

"Let me," she said.

She rolled the condom on, fingers shaking as she realized he was just as big here as he was everywhere else. She wasn't even aware she'd made a noise until he cupped her jaw and tilted her face up.

"Okay?" he said.

She licked her lips and nodded once.

That was all the encouragement he needed to tip her back on the bed, his body hot and heavy over hers.

Nothing slow or gentle this time.

His mouth demanded, and she gave. His hands stroked and kneaded, pulling responses from her that she'd never known she was capable of.

He pressed into her, hard, insistent, and she writhed against him, wild and wet and so desperate that she barely recognized her own keening cry as she went up in flames.

~

Lena wiggled into her dress and pulled up the side zip. She hadn't bothered with the bra, but panties…that was a different story. Without them, she still felt naked. She scanned the room, looking for the scrap of lace she'd abandoned in such haste.

"Do you have to go?" Adam's voice startled her. He'd been asleep when she slipped out of bed.

She glanced up now, to see him sitting up in bed, covers pooled over his lap. Her eyes rose to the broad expanse of chest that she'd explored with such enthusiasm earlier, and a shaft of heat speared through her. For a moment she almost succumbed to the temptation of climbing back into bed with him.

She forced herself to look away and resume the search for her missing clothes. "I can't leave my mother alone for long. The guests probably left a while ago."

In her peripheral vision, she saw Adam get out of bed.

"Looking for this?" he said, dangling her thong from an index finger.

She snatched it from his hand and turned her back to put it on, shimmying it up beneath the dress.

She yelped when Adam's hand settled on her hip.

"You could call her," he said, his voice low and intimate against her ear. His body brushed hers from behind, his pelvis pressing lightly against her. She could feel him hardening. "Say you've been...unavoidably delayed."

She closed her eyes, swallowed. "I left my phone at home."

His lips found the sensitive spot beneath her ear. "Use mine."

She wavered. Tilted her head slightly to allow him better access. Wondered if maybe she could stay just a little longer. Whatever post-dinner cleanup remained could wait. Surely her mother wouldn't be so foolish as to attempt it herself...?

Behind her, Adam shifted, widening his stance. His palm settled on her stomach, anchoring her in place as he pressed more firmly against her.

"Stay," he whispered.

She sighed and let her head drop back against his shoulder. Her hand, which had until now been hovering undecided in mid-air, settled atop his, their fingers interlacing. It wasn't clear who initiated the movement, but slowly their joined hands slid down, toward the apex of her thighs. Her tension mounted. Each breath became more ragged than the last.

"Adam…"

His fingers pressed between her legs, spreading her, and stroking her through the layers of silk. Could he feel how wet she was? She sucked in a breath as he adjusted the rhythm.

Maybe a little longer wouldn't hurt—

A faint buzzing sound in the background grew louder, more insistent.

Adam cursed beneath his breath. His fingers withdrew abruptly and Lena blinked at the sudden loss of heat as he moved away.

He grabbed his cell phone from the nightstand and read the incoming message. Another curse, and then he was dialing.

"Dr. Sterling," he said. "Someone paged?"

As he listened to the voice at the other end, his eyes met Lena's. "Sorry," he mouthed. "ER."

She nodded and shook off her bemusement. Smoothing down the dress, she spent several fruitless minutes searching for her bra before giving up. Adam was still on the phone when she retraced her steps to the front hall, where she'd left her keys and sneakers.

She was contemplating the etiquette of simply leaving, when he strode out of the bedroom, wearing the pants he'd discarded earlier and buttoning up a fresh shirt.

"Sorry about that," he said. "New consult. Patient in the ER with a lung mass and what sounds like a malignant effusion."

She nodded. "I have to get going anyway."

"Can you drop me at the hospital on your way?"

They'd taken her car earlier, since he'd walked to work as usual.

"Sure." She shifted from foot to foot as he finished dressing.

"Ready," he said, pocketing his phone and wallet, and clipping his hospital ID to the lapel of his jacket.

They made the three-minute drive in silence. Rather than parking in the physicians' lot, Lena pulled up to the ambulance bay leading directly to the ER.

"Thanks." Adam leaned over and dropped a casual kiss on her lips. "See you later."

She watched him stride through the double set of automatic sliding glass doors, tap his badge to the electronic panel at the staff entrance to the ER, and disappear inside.

~

The apartment was dark when she got home.

Lena flipped the light switch in the entryway and nearly jumped out of her skin when her mother's voice called out, "Where were you?"

Lena took a deep breath and slipped off her sneakers.

Her mother sat in an armchair in the living/dining room, wearing a loose house dress and slippers, her walker beside her.

"Hi, Ma." Lena went to the kitchen and turned on the lights. The dishwasher was running, and the counters were all clean. A glance into the dining room beyond showed that everything there had been cleared and put away as well. "You should have left everything. I would have cleaned up."

"You disappeared." Nina said, pushing the walker as she slowly entered the kitchen. "We waited, but it was getting late, and Sasha needed to leave. Masha insisted on cleaning. She said she could not leave me with a mess. Not in my condition."

Great. Lena sighed and poured herself a glass of water. *Guilt trip by proxy.*

"My thanks to Masha." Lena forced herself to smile. "How are you feeling, Ma? Do you want something to drink?"

"Why?" her mother said. "So I can run to the bathroom every half hour, all night long?"

Lena leaned against the counter. "I'll take that as a no."

"Where were you?"

"I told you," Lena said. "I had a patient to see."

"And it took you *five hours?*"

Lena shrugged.

"What am I supposed to tell Masha, after she went to so much trouble? And Sasha? What he must think of you! You will apologize for your rudeness."

"*My* rudeness?" Lena slammed the half-drunk glass down. "Not until dear Sasha apologizes for putting his hands where they don't belong."

"What? What are you talking about? Don't you turn your back on me! This discussion is not over."

Lena froze in the doorway and slowly turned to face her mother. "It *is* over, Ma. I'm seeing someone, okay?"

"What do you mean, seeing?"

Crap. Lena cursed her runaway mouth. But it was too late to take the words back. Besides, hadn't Adam volunteered himself as a contender for the position of son-in-law? As a joke, yes, but still. Desperate times and all that...

"We're dating," Lena said. And lest her mother get any ideas, she added, "Exclusively."

Her mother sank gingerly into a kitchen chair. "Why didn't you tell me? Why all the secrecy?"

Lena fluttered her hand. "It's early days."

"So, this boy you're dating—"

Lena stifled a snicker at her mother's description. Adam was young, but hardly a boy. Her cheeks heated at the memory of how he'd proven that earlier tonight.

"—what is his name? Where is he from? What kind of work does he do?"

Great. The inquisition was already starting. Was it any wonder she kept her personal life hidden from her mother? She shuddered at what her mother's reaction would be if she knew the *real* story.

Best to stick with the basics, and try to avoid getting in deeper. "His name's Adam Sterling," she said. "His family's from Connecticut. He's a doctor."

"Sterling?" her mother said. "What kind of name is that?"

"He's not Jewish, Ma, if that's what you're asking."

Her mother frowned, but didn't immediately rise to the

bait.

Lena sighed. "I'm tired. Do you need help getting to bed? No? Okay, then, I'm off. Goodnight."

Without waiting for her mother to ask any more questions, Lena turned on her heel and headed for the bedroom.

CHAPTER 12

Lena wasn't sure what to expect when she returned to work on Monday. Would Adam treat her any differently, now that they'd seen each other naked?

Did she want him to treat her differently? *No.* At least, not at work.

She still cringed at the awkward throat-clearing and pitying looks that came her way whenever the urologist she'd dated was mentioned in conversation. Maybe it was her own hypersensitivity, but it seemed like everyone at the hospital knew their history—an unfortunate byproduct of the very public way their relationship had played out, from the early days of flirting at surgical grand rounds, to the final crash and burn following a medical staff meeting. Considering the size of the medical staff, and the fact that Lena and the urologist served on some of the same hospital committees, it would probably be a while before she emerged from the shadow of that disaster.

She dreaded what might happen if she and Adam were seen treating each other as anything but colleagues. The hospital grapevine would go wild. She'd find herself the subject of salacious speculation yet again, especially once Adam left and she showed up with a baby bump.

But outside of work...? She'd be happy to get down and dirty with him again. A man who knew his way around a woman's body as well as Adam did? She'd totally trade in her battery-operated boyfriend if she could have *that* on tap.

And her mother thought they were an item. Sure, it might have started as a slip of the tongue. But if dangling Adam in front of her mother kept the matchmaking in check, Lena was all for continuing the charade.

She was sitting at her desk, plowing through her inbox, when Adam showed up. He wore scrubs and rubber clogs, and his hair still bore the imprint of a surgical cap. Messy had never looked so good.

"Hey," he said. "Glad I caught you before you left."

She smiled. "I was just finishing up."

"I texted you, but you didn't answer. A few of us are headed over to O'Brien's. Interested?"

Ugh. Her smile faded. He had to be kidding. Show up with Adam at the watering hole where much of the surgical staff congregated? That would be like announcing in the hospital newsletter that they were together.

She sifted through the papers on her desk, buying some time. Ah, there it was. Her errant iPhone. And Adam's text: *Dinner @ O'Brien's? 6-ish?*

"How about some takeout instead?" she said. "There's a great place just down the street from you."

There was a beat of silence. Had she misread the situation? Did Adam see Saturday night as a one-off? But then why bother inviting her to O'Brien's?

His smile allayed her doubts. "Give me ten minutes to shower and change, and I'll meet you in the lobby downstairs."

She used the time to skim her inbox for anything that couldn't wait, and called Cristina to ask if she could stay late. She could, but not past ten.

"That's fine," Lena said. That gave her four hours. A lot could be fitted into four hours. "Thanks, Cristina."

They stopped by one of her favorite Chinese takeout places. Her mother would no doubt turn her nose up at the menu, but for Lena, the restaurant's late hours and fast service were way more important than the fact that the food wasn't homemade. Plus, she'd had enough of cooking from scratch for a while.

"How was your day?" Adam said as they unpacked white cardboard containers at his kitchen counter.

"Good. Yours?"

"Great." He grinned and caught her around the waist, drawing her into kissing range. "And it's about to get better."

Oh, yes.

One kiss turned into two, then three, and the food was forgotten as they made their way to the bedroom, leaving a trail of discarded clothes along the way.

~

That day set the pattern for the weeks that followed.

Work, sex, food.

Sometimes they didn't even bother with the food. Other days, they ordered in, or Adam scrounged up something from the fridge after they'd sated their appetite for each other.

Lena found it increasingly difficult to compartmentalize, especially when just the sight of Adam in scrubs made her feel tingly and breathless. But she forced herself to behave with professional decorum, even when all she wanted to do was tear the thin blue material off of him and run her hands and tongue over every hard inch of his body.

His easygoing manner didn't help. Nor did the fact that he seemed oblivious to the boundaries she fought so hard to maintain.

At least in the OR she was able to filter out all distractions and concentrate on what was important, despite Adam's presence on the other side of the operating table whenever they scrubbed in on a case together.

"So when am I going to meet this mysterious boyfriend of yours?" her mother asked on one of the rare evenings Lena was home.

Lena paused in the process of foraging in the fridge for something that looked remotely appetizing. Between her mother's penchant for mayonnaise-laden salads and Cristina's meat- and cheese-heavy casseroles, the options were limited. She'd have to leave a new shopping list for Cristina tomorrow.

"Why do you want to meet him?" she said.

"Because you're spending so much time with him."

Lena sidestepped the question. "Yes, but you don't need me here. You have Cristina to help."

And Cristina was happy to earn extra overtime for staying late or spending the night. Especially now that Lena's mother had stopped threatening to fire her. The two had reached a grudging truce, though Nina still called Lena at work at least once a day to grumble about all the activity restrictions that the caregiver continued to enforce.

Lena opened a container of yogurt. "You want one, Ma?"

"No, thanks." Nina settled heavily at the kitchen table, parking the walker beside her. "You know, I can make yogurt that tastes much better than that."

"I know you can," Lena said. "Maybe once you're better…"

"I *am* better," her mother grumbled. "I'm so much better, I can move back home."

Lena raised a brow. "Really? What about stairs?"

"I've been doing stairs with the physical therapist for the last three sessions," Nina said. "You want to see? Come outside, I'll show you."

Lena watched her mother stand and wheel the walker toward the door. She dumped the empty container of yogurt and followed, surprised by the improvement from the last time she'd watched her mother do this less than a week ago.

Hanging onto the banister on one side and Lena's arm on the other, Nina managed the flight of stairs to the ground floor. After a short rest, she climbed back up and reclaimed the walker she'd left just outside Lena's apartment.

"There," she said. "The therapist said I can start using a cane."

Lena smiled and gave her a one-armed hug. "That's great.

There's a medical supply store a few blocks down. Why don't you go shopping with Cristina tomorrow? Find a cane that fits."

"Good," Nina said. "I look forward to sleeping in my own bed this weekend."

Lena hesitated. "You sure you're ready?"

"I'm ready."

And so, three weeks after moving in with her daughter, Nina made the return trip home. Cristina agreed to stay on as a live-in, though Nina protested the extravagance and claimed she was fine on her own at night. They compromised on a week of round-the-clock care, followed by daytime-only shifts, with a second caregiver to fill in for Cristina on the weekends. The final piece was signing her mother up for an emergency alert service.

"If anything happens and no one's around to help," Lena said, "all you have to do is press this button. A dispatcher will answer, day or night, and send help."

Her mother fingered the device. "It's a waste of money."

"Not if it gives you peace of mind," Lena said. "Think of it as an insurance policy."

"Insurance you can use," Nina said. "This thing I don't need."

Lena sighed. "Please, Ma. For *my* peace of mind, then, promise that you'll wear it."

"Fine, fine." Nina strapped the device around her wrist. "Now you can go. And don't forget to bring that boyfriend to visit. I'll make strudel and tea."

Lena escaped without agreeing to anything definitive, and spent the rest of the weekend reveling in the freedom of having her own space back.

With Adam's help, she restored her study to its former condition.

As they finished rearranging things, Adam grinned. "Ever had sex on a desk?"

Lena sauntered over to examine the item in question. "Not yet," she said, giving him a come-hither glance over her shoulder.

He promptly bent her over the pristine wooden surface and gave her a taste of what she'd been missing.

"Mm," she said later. "I can see why they call it *afternoon delight*."

He laughed and proceeded to spend the rest of the day and part of the night helping her inaugurate other places in her apartment where she'd never made love before, either.

~

A month after they first got together, Lena's self-indulgent bubble burst.

She was writing a brief op note in the PACU after her last case of the day, when Adam joined her at the nurses' station.

His hair was a shade darker than usual, still damp from the shower. He'd changed into street clothes and looked freshly-shaven. Over the last few days, Lena noticed that he'd taken to shaving after work. Because after their nightly exertions he no longer had time in the morning? Or in deference to her passing mention of whisker burn?

She breathed in the scent of his soap and tangy aftershave, more conscious of her own disheveled state after a full day in the OR. Despite the air conditioning, her skin felt hot and sticky.

"How about we eat out tonight?" he said.

She glanced around and turned back to the computer screen. "I still have to do post-op rounds."

"I can make a late reservation." He leaned against the counter beside her and pulled out his phone. "Would eight or eight-thirty work? Any food preference?"

"Adam—" she broke off as a nurse passed by and shot them a curious look. Waiting until they were alone again, Lena said in a softer voice, "Can we talk about this later? Not here?"

He looked up from the phone, as if finally picking up on her tension. Brow furrowed, he studied her, then slid the phone back into a pocket. "When are you free?"

She checked the time. "An hour? I can meet you at your place."

"Fine." He reached over to brush back a strand of hair that had come loose from her French braid and clung damply to her cheek.

Lena jerked back before he could make contact.

He froze, hand hanging in midair for a moment before he let it fall to his side.

She glanced around. No one appeared to be paying them any attention. She resumed her position in front of the computer, avoiding Adam's eyes. "Please," she said. "Not here."

Her fingers moved on the keyboard, typing gibberish, until she felt him move away. She waited until he was gone before letting out a breath and slumping back in her chair.

Later that night, she showed up at his door with takeout containers of lamb souvlaki and Greek salad, circumventing whatever plans he might have had to take her out.

"What's this?" he said, following her into the kitchen.

"Dinner." She set the food on the counter and crossed to the sink to wash her hands. "You said you like Greek food."

By now she was familiar enough with the layout to know exactly which cabinets and drawers held the dishes and silverware she needed.

Outside, the record high heat of the day still lingered, so instead of passing through to the patio where they usually ate, she set the kitchen table.

Adam stood in the doorway, arms folded over his chest. He watched her unpack everything, making no move to help.

Lena determinedly kept up a stream of inane chatter until he cut her off.

"What's going on, Lena?"

"I didn't have time to get wine," she said, opening the fridge. "But it looks like there's still some Pinot Grigio from yesterday. Unless you want water—"

"Lena."

She didn't see him move, but suddenly he was standing

behind her. One hand reached over her shoulder to shut the refrigerator door. The other settled on her hip, bringing her frenetic activity to a stop.

She swallowed. Her pulse skittered.

"Are you going to tell me?" he said. His fingers exerted gentle pressure, turning her around to face him. "Or am I supposed to guess?"

She stared at his chin. Up close, she could see that he'd nicked himself shaving—a tiny cut just below his lip.

The impulse to touch him was too hard to resist. She reached up to trace the nick with the tip of her finger, then let her fingers wander. A muscle in his jaw twitched beneath her fingers. He let out a shuddering breath and caught her hand in a firm grip, halting her exploration.

"Come on, Lena," he said, pressing her palm flat against his chest. She could feel the steady beat of his heart. "Tell the truth. Do I embarrass you?"

"What?" She tried to step back, but he encircled her waist with his other arm. "No," she said. "Of course not. But work is…separate."

"We weren't doing anything inappropriate."

"We were in the recovery room," she said. "There were people all around. You shouldn't be touching me."

"Oh, for Christ's sake." He dropped his hands and stepped back.

"I didn't mean now," she said, following.

He took another step back and shook his head. "This is crazy. You're happy to sleep with me, but you refuse to go out with me."

"That's not true," she said. "We went to that place near Cedars—"

"Once," he said. "And I'm not sure that even counts. You were upset about your mother, and I took advantage of the situation so you'd let me come with you."

"That's not what happened."

"That's exactly what happened," he said. "I'm not an idiot. It may have taken me a few times, but I finally glommed on to the fact that every time I suggest going somewhere public, you come up with some excuse or try to distract me." He waved toward the spread on the table. "That's what this is all about, isn't it?"

"Adam—"

"And if I so much as *breathe* in your direction when there are other people around, you act like I have Ebola."

She frowned. "I don't."

"You do." He raked his fingers through his hair. "I don't get it, Lena. Honestly. I mean, we have fun together, right? And I'm not just talking about the sex."

She wanted to reach out to him, tell him that he was right, they did have fun together. And no, it wasn't just about the sex. But she couldn't utter the words.

The gap between them widened until it was no longer just eighteen inches of space across a kitchen floor, but an unbridgeable divide brimming with mixed signals, cross-purposes, and regrets.

"I'm sorry. I can't do this." She looked around and blinked. It took her a moment to get her bearings. "I have to go."

She headed down the hall toward the entryway where she'd left her shoes and bag.

Adam followed. "So that's it? Is this your answer to everything, just cut and run?"

She whirled around, fists clenched. "I'm not the one who's leaving. *You* are, as soon as you're done with fellowship. So don't talk to me about cutting and running."

"That's different."

"Oh, yeah? How is it any different if the end result is the same? This—" she pointed between them "—was just a way for you to pass the time. But I live here. And when you're gone, I'm still going to be here, dealing with the fallout."

"What fallout?"

She shook her head and picked up her purse. "Forget it."

"Oh, no," he said, plucking the bag out of her hands. "You don't get to hurl accusations at me and then waltz out without explaining what the hell you're talking about."

"I'm talking about pregnancy, okay?" She glared at him. "I'm trying to get pregnant."

The bag slid from his grip and hit the floor. "What?"

"I don't mean right this second," she said. "But I'll be forty in January, so yeah, it's getting down to the wire."

He shook his head, stepped back. "You're sleeping with me just to get pregnant?"

"Don't be ridiculous," she said. "We've used condoms every time. And I didn't tamper with them, if that's what you're thinking. So relax."

"I'm not ready for kids."

"I know," she said. "You were never in the running."

"What?" He stopped retreating. "Then who the hell is?"

"I've got it narrowed down to a twenty-something engineering student from Texas who builds robots for fun, and a third-year medical student from Minnesota who wants to do medical mission work."

Adam stared at her. "You're having sex with other men?"

She glared back at him. They'd been practically living in each other's pockets for the last month. Adam knew her schedule better than she did. And she thought he knew *her*. Obviously they were both mistaken.

"Oh, sure," she said. "I've got nothing better to do between surgical cases."

He stopped and frowned. "If you're not sleeping with them, then what..."

"They're donors at a sperm bank." She propped her fists on her hips. "I'm seeing the gynecologist for testing this Friday. Then it's just a matter of deciding which donor, placing an order, and doing an IUI."

"A what?"

"Intra-uterine insemination."

His jaw dropped. "You're kidding."

"No."

"But...why?"

"Because I want a child," she said. "And this is the only way I'm likely to get one."

He stared at her. "But that's…crazy."

She stiffened. "It's not crazy. It's my life, my decision. I've been thinking about it for a while, and I've got it all planned out. You're not going to change my mind."

"I'm not trying to change your mind, dammit." He rubbed the back of his neck. "I'm just trying to understand."

She bit her lip. "I'm sorry. I never meant to dump this on you—"

"You just meant to dump *me*."

"No," she said. "This whole thing just got out of control. I wasn't even planning on sleeping with you. It just happened."

"Bullshit. Maybe the first time *just happened*. But after that? You wanted it as much as I did." He stepped closer and leaned down until she could feel his breath on her cheek. "You still want it."

"No."

"Yes." He wrapped his hands around her waist and drew her in, until she was pressed flush against him. "You do. You want me."

He gave her no chance to respond. His mouth covered hers and she moaned, helpless to stem the tide of heat and desire that rushed through her. She welcomed his tongue, his lips, his hands, every demanding stroke that imprinted him on her body.

Desperation overtook common sense, obliterated whatever good intentions she might have had. When he started undressing her right there in the entryway, his fingers clumsy in their attempt to undo, unbutton, unzip, she helped him, pulling the shirt from his pants, drawing the zipper down and cupping him through the cotton of his boxers. He tugged off the bits of clothing that got in the way, baring her from the waist down, fingers separating her slick folds before dipping inside.

She squeezed him and he cursed, shedding the boxers. Within seconds, his hands were gripping her ass, lifting her, and she wrapped her legs around him, giving him the opening he needed to thrust into her in one hard stroke.

She gasped and closed her eyes, hanging on to his shoulders

as he turned, still embedded deep inside her. Instead of heading down the hall toward his bedroom, he pressed her back against the wall and pounded into her as if his life depended on it. She hung onto him, panting, thighs tightening around him, both thrilled and appalled by the fierce need that rose inside her. It spiraled higher and higher, until she couldn't speak, couldn't breathe, couldn't do anything but cling to Adam as he drove into her, muscles flexing, breath harsh against her neck, his movements increasingly erratic, until he groaned and shuddered to a climax, triggering her own release.

For long seconds, there was nothing but the sound of their ragged breathing and the pounding of her heart in her ears. Aftershocks were still rippling through her body when Adam cursed and withdrew.

Lena opened her eyes. The abstract print she'd admired just a few weeks ago swam back into focus. Behind her, something was digging into her shoulder blade. The light switch, she realized, as Adam loosened his grip and she slid down, the movement inadvertently flipping the switch off and plunging them into semi-darkness. Her legs felt wobbly. If not for Adam's body still pressed against hers, his hands tightening around her waist, she might have slid right down to the floor.

"You okay?" he rasped.

She touched her tongue to her lips. They felt raw, swollen. She swallowed.

Something wet and sticky trickled down the inside of her leg.

Oh, no.

She reared back, her head knocking into the wall.

Adam pulled her into his chest, steadying her. "Hold on a minute," he said. "Let me check…"

He reached over her shoulder, switching the hall light back on. His fingers sifted through her hair, probing gently.

She winced. "Adam—"

"That was a pretty hard hit," he said. "Maybe you should sit down. I'll get you some ice."

"I'm fine."

He hesitated, then raised hand. "How many fingers?"

She blew out a breath. "Three."

He nodded and surveyed her half-dressed state.

She pulled the edges of her blouse together and snatched her panties from the floor, wishing she could escape to the bathroom to clean up and dress without an audience. A quick peek at him as she scrambled into her clothes showed that he was still watching, eyes narrowed.

"We didn't use anything," he said.

Her fingers slowed. "What?"

"No condom." He reached for his jeans and pulled them on commando-style, leaving the top button undone. "Are you on anything?"

She swallowed and finished tucking in her blouse. "I went off the pill a couple months ago."

His lips tightened. "What about fertility hormones?"

"No. The earliest appointment I could get was for this coming Friday." She spotted her bag a short distance away and picked it up, digging around inside until she found a hair clip.

"When was your last period?"

She hesitated, then finished putting up her hair in a haphazard twist. "I don't get periods. I haven't in years."

"You don't?" He frowned. "Why not?"

"Because I was doing continuous birth control. Skipping the placebo pills, going straight to the next pill pack."

"You said you stopped taking the pill two months ago."

She shrugged. "It can take a while to start ovulating again. Which is why I'll probably need Clomid to kick-start the process. I don't have time to sit around and wait for it to happen spontaneously."

"But what if it's happened already?" he said. "What if—"

"Adam, please. Let's just table this discussion." She hitched the shoulder bag higher. "I know my own body. And frankly, I have a better chance of getting hit by lightning than I have of getting pregnant from one encounter without a condom. So let's forget about it, okay? It's over, and you have nothing to worry about."

"Lena—"

"I'm serious," she said. "We still have to work together. It'll be a whole lot easier if we just pretend this never happened. Go back to the way things were before we…you know."

"Had sex?"

"Yes."

He rubbed the back of his neck. "But if you do get pregnant—"

"It won't be from this," she said. "And it'll have nothing to do with you."

A muscle in his jaw ticked. Finally, he nodded. "If that's what you want."

What she wanted was to roll back the clock and start the evening over again. Before things spiraled out of control. Before she and Adam called it quits. Before she realized how hard it would be to let him go, even if letting go was the right thing to do.

She wished that they'd met years ago, under different circumstances.

But they hadn't, and this was her reality.

"Goodnight, Adam." She turned to leave.

"Lena…"

She glanced back at him. "Yes?"

"You'll be okay to drive?"

"Yes." Stupid to feel so disappointed. After all, what had changed?

Nothing. And everything.

CHAPTER 13

"Remind me again," Dr. Goodman said. "How long have you been trying?"

"I haven't started," Lena said. "That's why I'm here. To get a fertility workup and talk about scheduling an IUI."

There was a knock on the door. One of the medical assistants came in and handed the obstetrician a note. He glanced at it, then looked at Lena over the rim of his reading glasses. "When did you say your last period was?"

"I don't remember," she said. "It's been years."

Which was exactly what she'd told him twenty minutes ago, when he was doing her pap. And that was after she'd already provided the same information on her intake questionnaire, and confirmed to the medical assistant that yes, her last period had been that long ago.

Was Dr. Goodman simply inattentive or forgetful? Either way, Lena was starting to have some serious doubts about the man, even though Rachel swore he was a miracle worker.

"All right," he said finally. "We'll need to do an ultrasound for dates, then draw some blood."

"Sorry?"

"You're pregnant, Dr. Shapiro," he said. "The only question is, how far along."

"But...I can't be." She closed her eyes, counted back the days. Eleven days since they'd had sex without a condom. Too early for her to even have missed a period—if she'd been having periods. And way too early for an ultrasound to show anything, even if the urine pregnancy test was positive.

Maybe they'd mixed up her sample with someone else's. She opened her eyes and glanced from Dr. Goodman to the note he'd placed on the desk. Even from this angle, she could see it had a label with her name on it, and a single handwritten plus sign.

Still, she asked, "Are you sure that's my result?"

He slid the glasses off and gave her a faintly amused look. "We'll do a blood test to confirm it," he said. "Between the quantitative HCG and the ultrasound, I think we'll be able to narrow down your due date."

A medical assistant ushered her back to an exam room across the hall and handed her a paper drape, with instructions to remove everything from the waist down. Dr. Goodman did the ultrasound himself.

After several minutes of silence, Lena turned her head to get a peek at the screen. Fuzzy gray and white images shifted in and out of view as the transducer moved over her stomach.

Uterus, ovaries, bladder.

"Let's see what the transvaginal ultrasound shows," Dr. Goodman said, wiping the gel off with a paper towel and switching to a different probe.

This time the images were a little clearer, and Lena saw it. A tiny little blob that couldn't have measured more than four or five millimeters.

"That's the gestational sac." Dr. Goodman froze the frame and enlarged it. "And here's the yolk sac and fetal pole."

Lena blinked. At eleven days, the ultrasound shouldn't have shown anything, even on transvaginal views.

Dr. Goodman's glasses glinted in the dark. "I'd say you're about six weeks along, give or take a few days."

"No," she breathed. "Impossible."

Six weeks—minus the two weeks that were tacked on by

convention to date pregnancies based on the last menstrual period—meant that she'd gotten pregnant *before* their one slip-up. Maybe even the first time she and Adam had gotten together.

She knew condoms weren't a hundred percent effective. But they'd been careful, and she was *thirty-nine*. Women her age didn't get pregnant by accident. They tracked their cycles with digital apps and ovulation kits, and shot themselves full of hormones to stimulate egg production, and paid tens of thousands of dollars for every high-tech attempt at baby-making.

She'd been prepared to do all that. What she hadn't been prepared for was an accidental pregnancy.

And what about Adam? She'd told him he had nothing to worry about. That their one little slip was unlikely to result in any consequences.

Technically, that was still true. It wasn't that final episode of wall-banging sex that had landed her in this position.

Six weeks. Unbelievable.

She left the OB/gyn suite and took the elevator down to the lobby.

"Which floor?"

She blinked, lifted her head.

There was a man standing near the front of the elevator, looking at her, his hand hovering over the floor button panel.

"Oh, sorry." She caught the doors before they slid closed. "This is me."

It took forever to find her car in the parking structure. Once she did, she slipped into the driver's seat and stared blindly through the windshield.

At some point, a security guard tapped on her window. "Is everything okay, ma'am?" he asked when she lowered the glass an inch.

"Yes, thank you." She glanced around. The garage was nearly empty. Where had all the cars gone?

The guard nodded and stepped away. "You have yourself a nice evening, ma'am."

"Thanks," she said. "You too."

She drove home on autopilot. Shedding her clothes, she brushed her teeth and climbed into bed, then spent half the night lying awake, staring at the ceiling.

Six weeks pregnant. Too early to make any decisions. Too early to know if the pregnancy was even viable. If she managed to get past the first trimester, with favorable results on genetic testing and repeat ultrasound, then she and Adam might have something to talk about.

Or not.

The circumstances hadn't changed just because she was pregnant. Adam had his future all mapped out, and it didn't include Lena or her child. As far as he was concerned, they'd made a clean break, leaving Lena free to pursue her baby dreams using donor sperm while Adam pursued his dream job on the East coast.

Why ruin his life over something she'd been planning to do on her own anyway? Adam could go his way, and she'd raise and nurture and love this child herself. Far better to do that than to risk exposing her child to resentment and possible rejection from a man who wasn't ready to be a father.

And if that logic failed to ease her guilt, she assured herself that she still had plenty of time to consider her options.

CHAPTER 14

The scorching heat lingered for weeks, fueling a record number of wildfires. Everyone seemed to know someone who was affected by the swathe of destruction that tore through California. Conversations revolved around the latest round of evacuations, recent efforts to help those displaced by the fires, and the poor air quality that was bringing record numbers of asthma and COPD exacerbations to the ER.

After a while, Adam tuned it all out. It wasn't that he lacked compassion for the victims. And he wasn't oblivious to the tension that his colleagues and other hospital personnel felt on hearing that the biggest fire was still only ten percent contained.

But he wasn't a local, and there were other things occupying his mind besides property damage in places he'd never even heard of.

He was in the ER finishing up a consult when the conversation around him turned from the fires to something new and much closer to home. *Lena.*

"—can you believe it? Right in the middle of surgery."

"At least she stepped away from the table before going down."

A new voice piped up, "I heard Dr. Harding was pissed."

"Probably worried about the liability," the first speaker snorted.

"What liability? He finished the case, and the patient's fine."

"Yeah, but Dr. Shapiro's still here in the ER…"

The voices faded down the hall.

Adam glanced around, then clicked out of his patient's chart and navigated to the ER census.

There she was, *Shapiro, Lena.* Trauma room 3.

His finger hovered over the mouse. He could be kicked out of his training program—or at least sanctioned and heavily fined—for committing a major HIPAA violation. And Lena sure as hell wouldn't thank him for violating her privacy. He hesitated for another moment, then logged off the computer and headed down the hall.

So what if it was in the opposite direction from the exit? And if this route happened to take him past trauma room 3, well, what of it?

They might not be sleeping together anymore, but they were still colleagues. No one could fault him for his concern over a colleague.

The glass door slid open and a nurse exited. Adam watched her disappear into another patient room.

Without a second thought, he slipped into Lena's room and ducked past the privacy curtain into the semi-gloom beyond. It took a moment for his eyes to adjust. The harsh overhead fluorescents were off, leaving only the ambient glow of under-cabinet lighting along the perimeter of the room.

Lena lay on a wheeled gurney with metal side rails, her eyes closed, lips dry, face leached of color. A blue hospital gown sagged loosely around her neck, and several layers of thin white blanket covered her from the chest down. An IV line dripped saline from a half-empty bag directly into her vein.

Above the bed, a monitor glowed green-on-black, tracing every heartbeat. Adam watched as the automatic cuff inflated, took a new measurement, then pinged and deflated. Lena's pulse seemed a little too fast and her blood pressure a little too low for comfort.

He must have made a noise, because Lena stirred and opened her eyes, then frowned.

"Hi." He snagged a rolling stool with his foot and pulled it close to the bedside. "How are you feeling?"

She licked her lips. "What are you doing here?"

"I was in the neighborhood…" He sat down and attempted a smile, but it fell flat. "What happened?"

Her fingers plucked at the sheets. "I got dehydrated."

"That's why you passed out?"

She hesitated. "Yes."

"You're not sick?"

"No." She brushed a limp lock of hair off her cheek. The rest of her hair fanned out on the pillow in wild disarray.

He glanced up at the monitor. Her numbers hadn't improved. "Your blood pressure's in the toilet."

"I always run low," she said. "And it's been hot."

"In the OR?"

"No. Outside. At home. My air conditioner's on the fritz."

"You weren't at home when you fainted," he said. "You were in the OR."

"I guess I overdid it." Her eyes flickered. "You know how it is. My last case ran over. Adhesions everywhere. So, no time for lunch…"

She looked so pale and fragile that he had to dig his fingers into his palms to keep from leaning over and wrapping his arms around her.

The privacy curtain swished open and a woman in pink scrubs entered, pushing a portable ultrasound.

"Hi, I'm Freda," she chirped, maneuvering the machine into place on Lena's right. "I'm here to do your ultrasound."

Lena shrank back against her pillow and jerked the covers up higher. "What ultrasound?"

"Your OB ordered it," Freda said, setting up her equipment as she talked. "He said he'll be down to see you shortly, but first he wants an ultrasound to make sure everything's okay."

Lena's eyes darted to Adam, then away. The beeping of her

heart monitor accelerated, triggering an alarm signal. Lena took a deep breath and pushed up to a half-sitting position.

Adam lurched forward, one arm outstretched to support her back, the other gripping the metal side-rail to keep himself upright.

"Breathe," he said, though he wasn't sure whom he was instructing—Lena or himself.

"Here." Freda reached over to lift the head of the bed. "Lean back and try to relax. Dad can stay with you if you want."

Lena's face turned ashen. "He's not—"

"For God's sake—" Adam squeezed her hand. "Breathe. Slowly. That's it, keep going..."

Freda backed away. "I'll get your nurse."

Adam ignored her, keeping his attention focused on Lena. Her fingers felt like ice. Fine tremors shook her body. "Come on, Lena, deep breath in...and blow it out."

The alarm stopped shrilling just as Freda returned with the nurse in tow.

"What's going on here?" the nurse said, glancing at the monitor, then at Adam, and finally at Lena. "Dr. Shapiro...?"

"I'm fine," Lena said.

Adam frowned. "She needs another blanket."

The nurse nodded and retrieved a blanket from a clean linen cart just outside the door. Adam forced himself to let go and step back, allowing the nurse to take charge.

Freda resumed her position in front of the ultrasound.

"I'll wait outside," Adam said.

Freda's gaze shifted between him and Lena. "This might take a while."

"I'll wait," he repeated.

He found an unoccupied spot behind the counter at the nurses' station, sufficiently out of the way to avoid interfering with the flow of traffic around him, but still close enough to have an unobstructed view of Lena's room.

She was pregnant. Why else would an obstetrician be seeing her in the ER and ordering an ultrasound? And Freda assumed

Adam was the father.

Christ.

He slumped in the chair and rested his head in his hands.

She'd gone and done it, just like she said she would. Straight from his bed to a fertility clinic for a date with some souped-up version of a turkey baster. No hesitation, not even a backward glance. And whatever fertility problems she'd anticipated had clearly proved no obstacle at all.

He was an idiot. Going over and over their time together, wondering what he could have done differently. Reaching for her in his sleep, then jolting awake because she wasn't there. Scouring the OR schedule for opportunities to first-assist on cases where she was listed as the surgeon of record, even when those cases had nothing to do with oncology.

And while he was busy making a fool of himself, hoping for an opening, however small, that might lead to a second chance, what was Lena doing? Moving on with her life. Without him.

Oh, she was polite enough at work. They still moved in perfect synchrony, as long as there was an unconscious patient strapped to an operating table between them. But the closer he tried to get to her, the more determined she seemed to freeze him out.

"Get over it, already," his sister Amanda told him, when he'd flown home for Labor Day weekend. "So the woman dropped your ass. So what? There are plenty of others out there who'd be thrilled to do the naked mambo with you, if you'd just stop moping and start looking around."

But I don't want any of those women, he wanted to say. *I want Lena.*

The problem was, Lena didn't want him. She'd cut him out of her life as if their time together meant nothing. And here she was, barely a month later, pregnant with another man's child.

What the fuck was he supposed to do now?

~

Lena imagined herself floating. Weightless, unencumbered. Warm water lapped at her as she drifted out to sea. Above her, the sky was a perfect cerulean blue, not a cloud in sight.

"How did it go?"

Her eyes snapped open.

Adam stood beside the bed. He'd shed the white coat and loosened the collar of his Oxford shirt. His hair looked as if he'd spent that last hour running his hands through it.

She licked her lips. "Fine."

He nodded. Shoved his hands in his pockets. "So who'd you end up choosing? The engineer or the med student?"

She gripped the side rail and took a deep breath, then slowly sat up. It took several seconds for the dizziness to pass. Unlike last time, Adam didn't rush forward to help.

Not that she expected him to. The fact that he'd returned at all, despite the awkward situation, surprised her.

She'd spent weeks avoiding him. Or at least attempting to. It wasn't always possible, especially when Lena's usual first-assist went on leave and Adam stepped in to fill the void.

Lena hid behind the surgical mask and used the presence of others as a buffer between herself and Adam. On the surface, she remained calm and professional. But inside, she was a maelstrom of churning emotions. Guilt. Anticipation. And most of all, fear.

Fear that her desire for Adam would overwhelm her good sense and she'd drag him to the nearest bed or desk or closet—anywhere private enough to indulge in a bit of pleasure.

Fear that once her pregnancy became apparent, Adam would see through her charade and connect the dots. Or worse, fear that he *wouldn't*.

She pulled her knees up beneath the covers and wrapped her arms around them. Confronted with Adam's point-blank question, she had a decision to make. Perpetuate the lie, or confess the truth?

The engineer or the med student, or...

"Neither," she said. "Turns out, you beat them to it."

For several moments, he didn't respond. Then, in a soft voice that belied the tension in his stance, Adam said, "Was that the plan all along? Use me to get pregnant, then make up some shit about an anonymous donor?"

Her eyes widened. "No," she said. "Everything I told you that night was true, I swear. How could you even think...?"

"When did you find out you were pregnant?"

She dropped her eyes to the covers. "The Friday after we broke up. I had an appointment with the OB for testing. It was supposed to be the standard fertility workup. But the ultrasound showed I was already six weeks pregnant."

"*Six weeks*...? Shit." He looked around, spied the rolling stool a few feet away, and sank down on it. "When were you planning on telling me?"

She bit her lip.

"I see." He clenched his jaw and looked down at his hands. The seconds stretched into minutes while he continued to stare hard at his palms, as if hoping to decipher some hidden meaning in the pattern of lines and whorls embedded there. Finally, he took a deep breath and curled his fingers into fists. "I'll want a DNA test."

"Adam...we don't need to do this. I mean, I'm perfectly capable of raising a child on my own—"

His head shot up. "Are you out of your mind? You think I'd abandon my kid just because you're in the mood to play supermom?"

"I'm sorry..."

"When's your next OB appointment?"

"Why?"

"So I can go with you." He stood. "We can do the testing then. I'll do a buccal swab, you'll give some blood—"

There was a knock on the metal door frame. The glass door slid open and Dr. Goodman entered.

"Dr. Shapiro." He pulled the privacy curtain closed behind him and approached the bed. "How are you feeling?"

Lena smoothed the covers over her legs. "Better, thank you. Sorry for all the fuss."

Dr. Goodman nodded and glanced at Adam. "I don't believe we've met," he said, extending a hand. "Nathan Goodman."

"Adam Sterling."

They shook hands, and Dr. Goodman turned back to Lena. "Your ultrasound was reassuring. Normal cardiac activity, measurements consistent with ten weeks. Have you been out of bed since they brought you here?"

"Yes, to the bathroom."

"Good," he said. "No more dizziness?"

She hesitated. "Only if I get up quickly. A second or two, then I'm fine. When can I get out of here?"

"Now, if you're ready," he said. "On one condition. You need to take better care of yourself. Slow down. Eat regularly. Hydrate well. Avoid standing too long on your feet."

Lena sighed. "You know I'm a surgeon, right?"

"Yes. But you're not the first surgeon to ever get pregnant. Others have done it and managed, and so will you. *If* you make your health a priority. Adjust your schedule, trade call, whatever it takes."

Lena frowned, but before she could say anything, Adam stepped in.

"You need to listen to the doctor, Lena," he said. Then he turned to Dr. Goodman. "Don't worry, I'll make sure she follows directions."

Lena glanced at him from the corner of her eye, but kept her mouth shut.

"Excellent." Dr. Goodman smiled. "I'll let the nurse know you're ready to go. She'll get you the discharge paperwork and take out your IV."

"Thank you."

He nodded. "I'll see you at your appointment next week."

The room remained quiet after he left.

Lena pressed the lever to lower one of the side rails. They'd taken her off the heart monitor earlier, so the only thing still tethering her in place was the IV. She turned to get off the bed, but before she could rise, Adam was at her side.

"Tell me what you need," he said. "I'll get it for you."

She gritted her teeth. "I don't need help. And what you said to Dr. Goodman was completely out of line."

"Really?" Adam folded his arms across his chest, blocking her way. "I saw your expression when he told you to take it easy. The world won't grind to a halt if you cut back your hours or take a day off once in a while."

"I know that," she said, glancing at the clock. "I'll make some adjustments. But right now I feel fine, and I still have patients to check on."

"Are you kidding me?" Adam dropped his arms to his sides, fists clenched. "After Goodman just read you the riot act? Christ, Lena, you're still hooked up to an IV."

"Which the nurse is about to remove. Dr. Goodman said I'm good to go. He didn't specify *where*."

"Because any reasonable person getting discharged from the ER would *go home*."

"I'll go home after I finish rounding," she said. "I did three cases today—three-and-a-half, if you count the one Erik took over—and those patients need to be seen."

He glared at her, then cursed, pivoted on his heel, and strode out of the room.

Lena stared at the privacy curtain that continued to sway in his wake.

Where was the feeling of triumph at having won the argument? She should have been glad that Adam was finally gone. But all she felt was deflated. So much for his promise to enforce Dr. Goodman's rules.

Not that she wanted him to. She was strong. Independent. And she had a job to do. So why was she still sitting in bed, instead of getting dressed?

She stood up and grabbed the IV pole, rolling it with her toward the counter where she'd seen a clear plastic bag stuffed with her belongings.

"Here we are," the nurse said, bustling in with a clipboard in one hand and what looked like folded scrubs in the other. "Why don't you go ahead and sit down? We'll go over your discharge instructions after I get that IV out. These are for you. Dr. Sterling said you'd need some fresh scrubs."

Lena felt the prickle of tears. Minutes later, she was alone again, pulling on the scrubs.

There was a cursory knock on the door, followed by the squeak of wheels.

"Your carriage, Princess." Adam pushed the wheelchair toward her.

She blinked. Those stupid tears threatened to spill over. Damned hormones.

"I can walk," she said.

"Not to your car," he said. "Hospital policy."

"But—"

"I called Dr. Harding," he said. "Your patients are all taken care of. He'll see the post-ops shortly. Said to tell you that the surgery went well, and that you should go home. Oh, and congratulations on the pregnancy."

"You *told* him?"

Adam raised a brow. "Was I not supposed to? He's your partner. He would've had to know eventually. I think he was relieved it wasn't something more serious."

"I should have been the one to tell him," Lena said.

"So, I saved you the trouble." He shrugged. "You can thank me later."

She glared at him. "You didn't say you were the…"

"Proud father?" he supplied. "I didn't have to. The man's not stupid."

"Oh God." She leaned against the counter and closed her eyes. "What am I going to do?"

Adam nudged the wheelchair closer. "You're going to sit down here and let me do the driving."

~

Lena did as he asked, not realizing that Adam meant to drive her all the way home.

But once he had her car keys, he refused to relinquish them, and she was too tired to argue. Though she'd never admit it, she was relieved. She closed her eyes and leaned back against the headrest.

Too soon, Adam was waking her up. "Come on," he said. "I'll help you pack."

She blinked. They were parked in front of her apartment building, and Adam was standing on the sidewalk, holding the passenger door open.

She accepted his hand getting out, then stopped as his words sank in. "What do you mean, pack?"

"Your air conditioning's broken, remember?" He hustled her through the outer gate and up the stairs. "So we're staying at my place."

"But it's cooler now," she said, ignoring the sweat that beaded along her hairline. "And the landlord promised to call someone to get the AC fixed."

"When?"

She shrugged.

"Exactly." He unlocked the front door and followed her in. "They're predicting highs in the nineties through the weekend. Pack whatever you'll need for the next few days. We'll reassess once your AC's back on."

Despite the evening drop in temperature, it was still uncomfortably hot. Lena's borrowed scrubs stuck to her skin. "I can stay with my mom."

He snorted. "Believe me, you'll be more comfortable at my place. And the commute's a hell of a lot shorter."

"Okay." She lifted her chin. "But I'm not sleeping with you."

"No problem," he said, lips twitching with a hint of a smile. "I have a guest bedroom."

And that was where he placed her suitcase an hour later, leaving her to unpack while he ordered dinner.

She sank down on the bed, atop the flowered comforter, and stared at the ceiling. Was it too late to say she'd changed her mind? That she'd much rather sleep in his bed than alone?

She missed having his arms around her. Missed the feel of

his bare skin against hers. Missed the sound of his soft, steady breathing when she closed her eyes at night.

Damn. If she felt this way after four measly weeks without him, what was she going to do when Adam left California for good?

CHAPTER 15

The following day, Lena was with her last morning patient when Rachel called. She wrapped up the visit, then took the call in her office.

"How are you feeling?" Rachel asked.

"Fine." Lena closed the door and headed for the couch. "Tired. You heard what happened?"

"Erik said you passed out and ended up in the ER. Is it true? You're really pregnant?"

"Yes." Lena toed off her shoes and stretched out. "I was going to call you later."

"We should go out and celebrate."

"Mm. I guess."

"You don't sound too enthusiastic," Rachel said. "I thought this was what you wanted."

"It was," Lena said. "It is. Maybe when I'm less tired, we can have a girls' night out."

"You bet," Rachel said. "How far along are you, anyway?"

"Ten weeks."

"Oh my God. And you kept it secret all this time?"

"It didn't feel real until a few days ago," Lena said. "Now, it's like my body finally woke up to the fact that I'm pregnant and decided to make up for lost time. I'm puking between every patient, and I'm so tired I can barely focus."

"Poor you," Rachel said. "But don't worry, it gets better once you hit the second trimester."

"That's what I hear."

"So what's with Dr. McHottie? The ER's still buzzing about him being here with you."

"Erik didn't tell you?"

"Tell me what?"

Lena closed her eyes. She appreciated Erik's discretion, but it was strange that hadn't confided his suspicions about Adam to his wife. Then again, he'd seemed more preoccupied lately, and having to fill in for Lena yesterday probably didn't help.

She took a deep breath and let it out slowly. "Adam's the father."

"What?" Rachel said. "No way. Are you serious? *He's* your sperm donor?"

"Yeah, I guess you could call it that."

"Wow. How'd you convince him to do it?"

"I didn't," Lena said. "It was an accident."

For several moments, Rachel didn't answer. Then, in a hushed tone, she asked, "You're sleeping with him?"

"Past tense," Lena said. "And anyway, this doesn't change anything. He's still leaving in March."

At least she assumed he was. He'd mentioned it last week, while they were standing side by side at adjacent faucets, scrubbing in for surgery. Apparently he'd set up his final rotation back East, at the institution where he was interviewing for a position.

"But you're not due until April," Rachel sputtered.

"I know."

"And you're okay with him leaving before you even deliver?"

"We're not together, Rach. That was never the plan."

"But plans change," Rachel said. "Don't you want a father for your baby?"

What she wanted was irrelevant. What she had was a man who'd temporarily inserted himself into the picture. What that meant for the future, she didn't know.

She sighed. "Rach, please—"

"And what about Adam? It's his kid, too. Doesn't he want to be involved?"

"He wants a DNA test."

"Well, of course. I mean, you were planning on doing that anyway, right? Advanced maternal age and all that."

"I'm not talking about checking for birth defects, Rach. I'm talking paternity testing."

"Oh." Rachel paused. "Is there any chance he's not the father?"

"No."

"I see." Another pause. "Well, I guess from a guy's perspective, it sort of makes sense. If it wasn't a planned pregnancy, and you're not really together..."

There was a knock on the door.

Lena opened her eyes to the sight of Adam entering. He had a tall disposable cup with a plastic lid in one hand and a brown paper bag in the other.

"Listen, Rach, I have to go. Talk later, okay?"

Adam set everything down on the low coffee table beside her. "How are you feeling?"

Lena sat up. "I've been better."

"Try the chamomile tea," he said. "It might help. And here, my sister swears by these." He pulled a box of saltines from the bag.

"Thanks." She sipped the tea and nibbled on a cracker. "You told your sister about this?"

"No." The sofa cushions dipped as he sat down beside her. "But Amanda's on her fourth pregnancy. Between her and Liz, I've probably heard it all."

For a while, they sat in silence as Adam watched her drink and work her way through a handful of saltines.

"You sure you don't want to go home?" he said. "I can see the rest of your patients today."

Lena swallowed down a fresh wave of nausea. "Shouldn't you be in the lab or something?"

He shrugged. "My schedule's pretty flexible. One of the perks of doing research."

"But you're not doing research full-time."

"True." He reached for the crackers and offered her another, then helped himself. "I talked with Erik. Explained that if I help lighten your work load, it'll take the pressure off of him as well. He seemed pretty understanding."

"Yeah, I bet."

"So, how about taking the afternoon off? You can put up your feet, watch some news..."

Despite the light tone, Lena could feel his concern as he studied her.

He'd made breakfast that morning, which she promptly vomited up in the toilet while Adam knelt beside her, holding her hair out of the way. When there was nothing left to bring up, and the dry heaving had finally subsided, he offered her a damp washcloth and a glass of water.

She felt so wiped out that she barely protested when he drove them to work and told the medical assistants to direct any last-minute consults or add-ons his way.

Despite recurrent bouts of nausea and vomiting, Lena got through the morning.

She was used to powering through adversity. In a crisis, she was the one people relied on. The one who made sure, after their father died, that her sister got fed and did her homework and brushed her teeth before bed. The one who ran interference between her sister and their mother after Zhanna dropped out of school to play house with a man their mother refused to even acknowledge until after the birth of their second child. It was Lena who dealt with their mother's hip fracture, and all the arrangements that had to be made for her post-operative care.

Lena wasn't used to being coddled herself. It felt oddly disorienting to have someone hover over her, ready to rush in and rescue her at the slightest sign of trouble. Especially when that someone was Adam, whom she'd pegged as too young and carefree to handle the role.

"I'm fine," she said now, even as a tide of fatigue threatened to pull her under.

He gave her a final assessing look before nodding and getting up. "There's some yogurt and cut-up fruit in the bag," he said. "I'm going over to the lab for an hour or two. Call me if anything changes."

~

Adam did his best not to crowd Lena, even though some atavistic impulse urged him to grab her and carry her off. She needed to rest and recover, far from the pressure cooker of work and the prying eyes of colleagues and staff.

He wouldn't mind having a break, either.

The past few days—weeks, if he was honest—had ripped apart the familiar landscape of his life. He'd plunged from the euphoric high of a new relationship to the miserable low of being dumped, then segued into a brief period of optimism fed by the irrational hope of rekindling his romance with Lena.

And then there was the shock of her pregnancy. He was still reeling from it, though his initial anger and feelings of betrayal had morphed into fierce possessiveness. Even without the DNA evidence, he knew deep in his bones that Lena's child was his. And, by extension, so was Lena.

She might not see it that way, but Adam figured that with time and care, she'd come around.

Granted, this wasn't exactly how he'd envisioned his own life, back when he was much younger and way more arrogant.

The product of three generations of wealth and social stature, Adam had grown up believing he had ultimate control over his own destiny. He was, after all, a Sterling, even if he'd chosen a career in medicine rather than going into the family business. While his father and uncles, sisters and cousins, all joined Sterling Therapeutics, Adam powered through medical school, surgical residency, and now a fellowship in surgical oncology.

Once he had his degree in hand and his training completed,

he'd planned on returning to the East coast to join a top-tier cancer center. Then, and only then, would he turn his attention to finding a woman of similar background and pedigree, who'd fit into his lifestyle and get along with his family. They'd marry, buy a house close, but not too close, to his parents and siblings, and start producing the next generation of Sterlings.

How smug he'd been, assuming that the future was his to dictate. How ignorant, thinking that love and children could be scheduled as precisely as a dinner date or an appointment with the family lawyer.

He knew better now. Lena proved how easily and quickly physical attraction could flare into a life-altering conflagration, reducing all his plans and assumptions to ashes, clearing the way for a new reality.

His new reality, and hers. *Theirs.*

~

Monday evening, Lena wandered into the kitchen while Adam was cooking.

"My landlord left a message," she said. "The air conditioning's fixed."

Adam stilled for a moment, then turned off the burner. Clouds of steam billowed into the air as he drained the pasta. "Dinner's almost ready. Would you mind setting the table?"

She set her phone down on the counter. "I can go home now," she said as she arranged plates and silverware on the kitchen table.

He sprinkled the pasta with salt and olive oil. No garlic or tomato sauce, since they seemed to make Lena's nausea worse. He handed her a bowl of lightly dressed salad greens and nudged her toward the table. "Dinner first."

They ate in silence. Adam watched for any signs of incipient illness, but for once she didn't seem on the verge of fleeing to the restroom.

He waited until she was finished eating before saying, "Why not just stay here, with me?"

Her water glass clinked against the plate as she set it down. "I want to go home."

"Why?" Adam asked. "This place is more convenient. Closer to the hospital."

"I know, but—"

"You shouldn't be alone." He rose to clear the table. "Want some chamomile tea?"

"I've been on my own for twenty years," she said. "I think I can handle it."

"Not in your current condition." He filled the electric kettle and turned it on. "This is the first meal you haven't thrown up in days. And half the time you look like you're falling asleep on your feet. There's no way I'm letting you get behind the wheel—"

"*Letting* me?" She stood up, one hand clutching the back of the chair, the other balled into a fist at her side. "I don't need your permission."

He sighed and pinched the bridge of his nose. "I know. I'm sorry. It's just...I worry, okay? I need to know you're safe. If you want to go home, fine, I'll go with you. Just give me a chance to finish cleaning up and pack a few things—"

"Wait." Her eyes narrowed. "What do you mean, go with me?"

"Lena, sweetheart, we're in this together. If you move back to your place, I'm moving in with you."

Her mouth fell open. "You can't just move in with someone without being invited."

"So invite me."

"No." She folded her arms across her chest. "No way."

"Why not?"

Her mouth tightened. "My apartment's not big enough for both of us."

"Your mother stayed there for three weeks."

"Yes, but now she's gone, and the study is back to being a study, with no extra bed..."

"So I'll share your bed," he said. When her expression darkened, he sighed. "Or I could take the sofa."

Her eyes swept him from head to toe. "You'd be uncomfortable."

He shrugged. "If that's your only objection..."

"Fine," she said. "I'll stay here. But I'll need to pick up some more things."

"No problem." He turned back to the kettle to hide his smile. "Let's have some tea first, then I'll drive."

CHAPTER 16

As the day of her follow-up OB appointment approached, Lena got increasingly antsy.

"Are you feeling sick?" Adam asked Thursday evening, after ten minutes of watching her push the same piece of lettuce around her plate.

"What?" She blinked and glanced up.

"You're not eating."

She stabbed at the lettuce leaf, took a bite, and chewed. "About tomorrow…"

"Yes?"

"You don't have to come with me."

Adam raised a brow. "They'll need some DNA from me, too."

"You can stop by the lab for five minutes to do a buccal swab," she said. "No need to wait with me for an hour or two or however long I'll be there."

"Are you trying to get rid of me again?" he said.

She flushed. "No. I'm just saying it's a waste of your time, that's all."

He set down his knife and fork and regarded her steadily. "I thought we'd gotten past this stage."

"What stage?"

"Being embarrassed if someone happens to see us together."

She stared at her plate. "You don't understand…"

"So why don't you explain it to me?"

The silence pulsed between them.

Finally Lena cleared her throat and looked up. "I was planning to have a child on my own," she said. "Career women my age do it all the time. People *respect* that. But getting knocked up and then abandoned by some guy who's just passing through? That's just stupid. Or desperate. Or both. I'd never live it down—" she broke off to glare at him. "What? Why are you laughing?"

"Because what you just said is ridiculous." He shook his head, still grinning. "I'm not '*some guy who's just passing through*' and I sure as hell don't plan on abandoning you."

"You're leaving for Sloan Kettering."

"Not until March," he said. "And you could always come with me."

Her heart stuttered. Come with him? To do what, exactly?

"You have to admit," he continued, "it would solve the problem."

She wasn't sure if it was his word choice or breezy tone that set her off.

"There wouldn't *be* a problem if you backed out now." She pushed away from the table and marched over to the sink, where she dumped her plate and utensils before turning back to face him. "I don't need a DNA test to prove what I already know, and I don't need your help—financial or otherwise—to raise this child. So what's the point of going with me? What's the point of doing a DNA test at all?"

He got up, all laughter gone. "The point is, I will not be cut out of my own child's life. What will it take to keep that from happening, Lena?" He stalked toward her. "You tell me, and I'll do it."

He stopped in front of her and leaned forward, resting his hands on the granite counter on either side of her waist, caging her in.

"Tell me," he repeated. His breath stirred the fine hairs along her temple.

She tilted her head back, meeting his gaze. His eyes darkened, a thin rim of iris engulfed almost entirely by pupil.

"Adam…" She inhaled the faint tang of his cologne, and a familiar ache settled in her pelvis.

His eyes dropped to her lips. "Yes?"

Was it her imagination, or had the space between them narrowed?

"I can't," she whispered.

"You can, Lena." His lips grazed her brow. "Tell me what you want."

What did she want? She couldn't think. Couldn't do anything but feel the heat coming off him in waves, the tension in his muscles as his hands closed around her waist, thumbs making small circular movements over her belly.

She closed her eyes, trying to recapture the thread of their conversation. What did she want?

Longing swirled through her. "I want…"

His hand shifted, grazing the underside of her breast. Her nipples beaded beneath the thin cotton of her shirt and bra, and she sucked in a breath, letting her head fall back.

"Yes?" His lips found her neck. "What do you want?"

She shivered beneath the hot glide of his tongue. "You," she said, clutching the fabric of his shirt. "I want you."

Afterward, she couldn't recall who moved first. Not that it mattered. The end result was same: a mutual abandonment of inhibitions as they came together in a rush of heat. Lips melded, tongues thrust and parried, fingers tangled in their haste to strip off clothing that had suddenly become superfluous.

The granite was cold and hard beneath her, but Adam's hands and mouth warmed her so thoroughly that by the time he entered her, she was oblivious to everything but the feel of his skin against hers and the slick glide of his body inside her.

With each thrust, the tension mounted. His fingers dug into her hips as he plunged deeper, harder, faster.

She tightened around him, gasping, her muscles quivering. "Oh, God…"

When he tried to pull back, she wouldn't let him.

"Lena," he rasped. His hand moved, sliding between them. His thumb found her clit and rubbed, tiny circles that became ever more erratic. "I can't…oh, fuck…"

He jerked inside her, once, twice, and then stilled, his face buried against her neck.

The discomfort of lying on a granite counter-top finally penetrated, and Lena shifted. Adam stirred and groaned, then pushed himself off her.

She shivered at the loss of his body heat.

"Sorry," he muttered, lifting her down to the floor before removing what was left of his shirt and wrapping it around her. "Are you okay?"

She swayed and leaned against him, clutching the edges of the shirt closed with one hand, and pressing the other against her stomach. "Oh, God. I think I'm going to be sick."

He didn't hesitate, sweeping her up and to the bathroom before she could say another word. He deposited her beside the toilet, pulled a towel from the hook on the back of the door, and spread it on the floor in front of her.

She knelt on it and closed her eyes. A drawer opened and she could hear Adam rummaging inside. There was the sound of running water.

"Here," he said.

A damp washcloth appeared in her hands. She swallowed and buried her face in it.

"Keep breathing," he said, hunkering down beside her. His fingers smoothed her hair back into a loose tail. There was a series of clicks and then a soft curse. "How do you work this thing?"

She lifted her head and winced.

"Sorry." Adam let go of her ponytail and fumbled with a large claw-tooth clip, trying to keep it open. "I think it's broken."

"Let me." With a few deft movements, she twisted her hair

out of the way and secured it with the clip—just in time.

He hovered over her until she felt well enough to rinse out her mouth and brush her teeth. Taking down her hair and brushing it sapped the rest of her energy. She couldn't even summon a token protest when Adam carried her to his bed rather than the one she'd been sleeping in for the past week.

He slipped a fresh t-shirt over her head. From the size of it, it had to be one of his.

She stirred when the mattress dipped behind her.

"It's okay," he murmured. "We're just sleeping."

She closed her eyes and relaxed into his body as it spooned hers from behind, his palm resting on her still-flat belly.

~

The visit to Dr. Goodman's office went smoothly.

Adam stood beside the examining table where Lena lay, stomach exposed, an ultrasound probe pressing against her over-full bladder. His fingers found hers and squeezed as the rapid whoosh-whoosh of their baby's heartbeat filled the room. She glanced up at him, but his eyes were glued to the monitor, where an ultrasound technician was measuring the crown-rump length and thickness of the nuchal fold.

After a medical assistant finished swabbing Adam's cheek and drawing Lena's blood, Dr. Goodman rejoined them.

"Looking good," he said. "I should have the test results in seven to ten days. Do you have any questions?"

Lena shook her head no.

"I do," Adam said. "About Lena's weight loss…"

Dr. Goodman reassured Adam that yes, some women did lose weight in the first trimester, and no, Lena didn't need a prescription anti-emetic, and this did not qualify as hyperemesis gravidarum, and there was nothing more to do at this point than what they were already doing.

They drove home in silence.

"I need a shower," Lena said as soon as they walked through the door.

Adam nodded. "Take your time."

She did. But half an hour later, she wished she hadn't.

"What the...?" She stared around the empty guest room. Her bag was no longer on the dresser top where she'd dumped it a short while ago. The rumpled sundress that she'd flung over the back of a chair was also missing, as were the clean yoga pants and t-shirt she'd left on the bed. A quick check of the dresser drawers and closet yielded the same result: all her things were gone.

She rushed down the hall, calling Adam's name.

"What's wrong?" He caught her just before she barreled into him, on the threshold to his bedroom. "Are you okay? What happened?"

"My things—" she said, and then stopped. Because in his hand was the cell phone she'd left on the bedside table in the guest room. She pulled away and glanced past him, into the bedroom beyond.

Her bag sat on the steamer trunk at the end of Adam's bed. The yoga pants and shirt were folded neatly atop the covers on the left side of his bed, where she'd slept the night before.

"I transferred everything here." He ushered her inside and placed her phone on the nearest nightstand. "Now that we're back together—"

"What?" She stopped and stared at him. "Where did you get that idea?"

"Last night..." he trailed off, brow furrowed.

"Last night was a one-off," she said. "I don't know what got into me—"

"*I* did," he said. "And I'd like to do it again. And again. And—"

"Stop. Please." She backed away and wrapped her arms around herself, hands gripping her elbows.

"What's wrong?"

She shook her head. "This. All of it. You can't make unilateral decisions and expect me to fall in line."

"Unilateral?" he said. "There was nothing unilateral about last night. You were right there with me. In the kitchen. In bed."

She closed her eyes, trying to block out the images his words evoked. But flashes of memory kept intruding. Adam, fully aroused, kneeling before her on the kitchen floor, his big hands steadying her hips as he licked and sucked her into a state of complete abandon, before finally surging to his feet and lifting her onto the counter for the wild finale. The nipple-puckering shock of cold granite against heated skin. The force of him driving into her while his fingers played with her, speeding them both toward climax.

Her breasts tingled, nipples tightening beneath the toweling robe. *Focus on something else.*

She opened her eyes. Her gaze flitted about, finally settling on the nightstand, where Adam had deposited her iPhone.

"What were you doing with my phone?" she asked.

He frowned, following her gaze. "What does that have to do with—"

"Please," she said. "Just answer the question."

He studied her for several moments, a muscle in his jaw twitching. "Your mother called," he finally said. "She's expecting us at seven tomorrow night."

"*What?*"

"She invited us to dinner."

"And you couldn't say no?"

"She's your mother." Adam shrugged, as if that explained everything. "We'll talk, eat, tell her she's going to be a grandma. Unless she knows already…?"

"God, no." She wasn't ready for a confrontation with her mother. And that's what it would come down to. Lena on one side, her mother on the other, and a big stinking argument over bad judgment and poor life choices in between.

She'd prefer if Adam remained a disembodied name. The phantom boyfriend she could brandish at her mother like a talisman to ward off the evil eye whenever Nina threatened to turn matchmaker. Better that than offering up a live target for her mother's barbs.

"Come on, Lena," Adam said, moving closer. "How bad

could it be?"

"Does *your* family know?" she shot back.

"I'll tell them in a couple weeks, when I see them."

"Oh." Her outrage fizzled a little. "Are they coming to visit?"

"No," he said. "I'm going to New York to interview at MSK. I'll swing by Westport on my way back."

Lena's muscles tightened. She wasn't even aware that her nails were digging into her elbows until Adam reached for her. His fingers traced hers, his touch light, coaxing.

"Come with me," he said. "Take a little break. Meet my family."

She shivered, but didn't pull back. "Adam..."

"No need to be nervous," he murmured. "Everyone will love you."

Her pulse skittered. The words echoed in her head. *Everyone will love you.*

She took a deep breath. *Don't be an idiot.* He meant his family. His parents, his siblings.

Not himself.

And yet, she couldn't help but wish...

His lips brushed her temple. "What do you say?"

He was trying, despite all the roadblocks she'd erected to keep him away. And it wasn't just about the sex. He'd told her that weeks ago. She hadn't believed him then, but she was starting to now.

She couldn't imagine any of the other men she'd dated holding her hair back while she retched into the toilet, day after day after day, ad nauseum. Couldn't imagine them cooking for her, or holding her through the night, or pestering her obstetrician out of concern that she'd lost yet another pound.

Any of those other men would have abandoned the effort long before now.

But not Adam.

Whatever he was offering might not be love, and it might not be forever, but she'd be lying to him and to herself if she continued to insist that she didn't want it.

"Okay," she said. "We'll have dinner with my mom tomorrow."

"And dinner with my folks in two weeks?"

"I'll need to talk with Erik," she said. "Two weeks isn't much time to arrange coverage."

"But you'll try," Adam said.

"I'll try."

He cupped her cheeks with his hands and pressed a gentle kiss to her lips. "Thank you."

She covered his hands with her own and leaned into his embrace. "I'll need some closet space if I'm staying here."

His lips curved up. "Sure thing," he said. "Take as much space as you want."

CHAPTER 17

When they arrived at Nina's house the following night, they were greeted by pandemonium.

Sarah and Gabby, Lena's nieces, were in the living room, arguing over whose turn it was to control the remote, while the television blared in the background. They stopped the moment they saw Lena and rushed toward her. Sarah, who was twelve, slowed down on noticing that Lena wasn't alone. But her younger sister barreled on, launching herself into Lena's arms so hard that Lena staggered back, bumping into Adam, who was right behind her.

"Whoa," Lena laughed, catching her breath and returning the hug. "You look like you've grown two inches since the last time I saw you."

Gabby pulled back. "I'm almost as tall as Sarah, and she's in seventh grade! Grandma says it's because I eat all my vegetables and Sarah doesn't—"

"I do," Sarah interrupted, edging closer. She peeked at Adam, then ducked behind a curtain of long blond hair. "Hi, Aunt Lena."

"Hi, Sarah. How is ballet?"

The girl shrugged. "Okay."

"Did you bring any presents?" Gabby said.

"Not this time," Lena laughed. "I didn't know you'd be here."

"Sarah, Gabriella, enough." Lena's mother wiped her hands on a stained apron and ushered the girls back to the living room, whispering a few words to Sarah before returning. "Sorry. Come in, come in. You must be Adam. Dinner will be ready soon. Have a seat, there, in the dining room. Lena, pour some wine. I'll be in the kitchen."

"Wait," Lena said. "You invited Zhanna and Patrick?"

Her mother's mouth tightened. "No." She glanced briefly at Adam before turning back to Lena. "Get your friend settled, then come help me in the kitchen."

The smell of fried onions and charred meat hit Lena before she even stepped into the kitchen. She swallowed a wave of nausea and glanced around. Every available surface appeared to be covered with food in various stages of preparation. Cristina was washing dishes. She glanced up when Lena entered and greeted her with a brief smile before turning back to her task.

Nina stood at the stove, stirring something in a pan.

Lena stopped a short distance away. "What's going on, Ma?"

Nina turned off the burner. "Your sister is here with the girls," she said in Russian. "They'll be staying for a while. Do you mind getting me a serving dish for this? In that cabinet over there."

Lena did as her mother asked. "Did something happen?"

Nina concentrated on transferring the potato-mushroom-onion sauté from frying pan to serving dish. "Try it. It might need salt."

"Ma…"

"I told her that man was no good for her, didn't I? And now—" Nina shook her head. "How is she going to get back on her feet without an education? She should have finished her degree, like I told her, instead of relying on that…" She pursed her lips. "You should talk to her. She's in her old room."

"Now?"

"Now."

Lena knocked softly on her sister's door. There was no response. She opened it. "Zhanna?"

In the darkness, she could barely make out the outline of the furniture. She felt along the wall for the light switch.

"Don't," her sister said.

But it was too late.

Lena gasped. Her sister lay curled on her side in bed, her back against the wall, her bruised face almost unrecognizable. One eye was blackened and swollen shut. Her lip was cut and puffy.

"Oh, God." Lena rushed to the bed, kneeling beside her sister. "What happened?"

"Go away."

"Zhanna—"

"Please." Zhanna closed her good eye. "Just leave me alone."

Lena stared at her for a moment, then rose and turned off the light. It took a few moments for her eyes to adjust. She made her way back to the bed and sat down on the edge, careful not to jostle her sister.

Beyond the closed door, Lena could hear the faint sounds of canned laughter from the television. The rise and fall of her nieces' voices as they resumed bickering. Whatever had happened to their mother, at least the girls seemed unharmed. Though now that she thought about it, they'd both been more subdued than usual.

Zhanna stirred. "Why are you still here?"

"I want to help." Lena hesitated. "Have you been to a doctor?"

"No."

"Do you want me to…take a look?"

"No." Zhanna shifted again. "Nothing's broken. I'll be fine in a few days."

"How do you know?"

In the ensuing silence, Lena felt her muscles tightening as her imagination ran riot. Surely if her sister was in trouble, she would have said something? Appealed for help?

"Zhanna…" She hesitated, unsure of how to proceed. "Has this happened before?"

Her sister made a soft sound, like an animal in distress. Lena reached out, her fingers hovering over the dark shape of Zhanna's head before moving gingerly to rest on the rounded curve of her shoulder. They stayed that way for a long time, without moving, their breathing and Zhanna's occasional sniff the only sounds in the dark room.

"He promised it wouldn't happen again," Zhanna finally said in a soft, raspy voice. "He works so hard. Business has been tough—"

"That's no excuse." Lena paused, dreading the question, and yet knowing it had to be asked. "What about the girls? Has he ever—"

"No," Zhanna said. "He never touched them. He's a good father."

"Not if he beats their mother. How long has it been going on?"

Zhanna's shoulder moved in a half-shrug.

"You should have told me," Lena said. "I would have helped, dropped everything and—"

"Saint Lena." Her sister's mocking tone stung.

"I understand you're upset," Lena started.

"Don't." Zhanna cut her off and scooted up in bed, dislodging Lena's hand. "I know I've made a mess of things, but I'm dealing with it, okay? I don't need you to point out my mistakes."

"I wasn't…" Lena stopped and took a deep breath. How had their relationship deteriorated to this extent?

Sure, they weren't close like some sisters were. Their age difference was too vast, and their paths too divergent. Whatever common interests and experiences they might have had before didn't stand a chance after Patrick came along.

When Zhanna got pregnant and announced she was dropping out of school to get married, Lena tried to dissuade her. But her arguments fell on deaf ears.

"Patrick wants to take care of me, of us," Zhanna insisted. "And besides, what am I going to do with a bachelors in comparative literature, anyway?"

"You can use it as a stepping stone to any number of careers," Lena told her. "Or you can go to grad school."

Zhanna shrugged her off. "You're just jealous."

And Lena had to admit there was some truth in that accusation. Zhanna glowed with the happiness of new love and motherhood. She had the perfect husband, the perfect children, the perfect life. She didn't have to deal with the stresses of building a career that demanded everything and left time for nothing.

Was it any wonder that Lena sometimes envied her? Or that she resented how often Zhanna used her husband and children as an excuse to avoid helping with their mother?

Now, in retrospect, Lena realized that she'd let her own prejudices blind her to what had been there all along. Little clues that all was not so perfect in Zhanna's life. She should have taken the time and effort to look beyond her sister's prickly attitude. Beyond the flimsy excuses for why Zhanna couldn't run an errand for their mother. Beyond the offhand explanations for why her sister was moving so stiffly—Pilates, or Orange Theory, or whatever exercise fad she was supposedly trying.

Lena forced herself to push aside the memories and guilt. "What are you going to do now?" she asked.

Zhanna sighed. "I don't know. Mom's letting us stay here for a while. Until I get my head together."

"You're not thinking of going back to him...?"

"No," Zhanna said. "No. Not this time."

Lena bit her lip. Damn Patrick. "Will you and the girls be safe here?"

"Yeah. He wouldn't..."

Lena waited for her to continue, but Zhanna remained silent.

"Do you have a good lawyer?" Lena finally said. "I could ask around, if you want."

"Thanks. I'd appreciate it." Zhanna hugged her knees to her chest beneath the blanket. "I'm sorry for ruining your evening."

"You didn't."

"Mom said you were bringing someone. A new boyfriend."

"His name's Adam." Lena rose and smoothed down her skirt. "I should probably make sure Mom hasn't scared him off."

"You won't mind if I sit this one out?" Zhanna said. "I'm not up for company."

Lena glanced toward the door. "I can send him home, if you want. We can have dinner, just us. You, me, Mom, and the girls."

"Thanks," Zhanna said. "But no. You go out there. I'll meet him some other time, okay?"

~

She found Adam in the living room sitting between the two girls, the three of them watching a superhero remake on TV.

"Everything okay?" he said, glancing up as she entered the room.

She shook her head and mouthed "Later," then took a seat beside Gabby on the sectional sofa. The girl snuggled up to her and whispered, "Watch this, Aunt Lena. That's the good guy, in red. He's going to clobber the bad guy—see, that's him, right there."

An hour later, they were seated at the table, passing around bowls of *vinigret* and *salat olivier* and plates of sliced *kielbasa* and black bread.

"So, Adam, tell me about yourself," Lena's mother said. "Lena says you're a doctor."

Lena gripped her fork. Another two hours, three at most, and she'd be back home, wrapped in Adam's arms.

For now, she just needed to get through the meal without throwing up or bursting into tears.

~

Lena buckled her seatbelt and looked at Adam, trying to gauge his mood.

He hadn't said anything since they left her mother's house, if you didn't count the noncommittal grunt he'd made in response to her comment, "I thought that went well."

He hadn't even touched her, other than to help her into the passenger seat.

At the moment, he was fiddling with the air conditioning vents.

They were pulling onto the 10 West when she broke the silence. "Adam…"

He glanced at her. "Am I allowed to talk now?"

She flushed. It was true, every time he'd tried to tell her mother their news, Lena cut him off and changed the subject. After a few puzzled looks, he'd given up and let her direct the conversation. It worked only because her mother was too distracted by the additional two guests at the table—and likely by concern over the third guest who hadn't joined them.

"I'm sorry," Lena said. "Tonight was just…bad timing."

"You want to tell me why?"

She did.

"Sonofabitch," he said when she finished. "She needs a restraining order. And a gun, so she can shoot the bastard if he ever shows his face."

Lena sighed and leaned back against the headrest. "What she needs is a good divorce attorney. I promised to find her one."

"You think she'll be safe at your mom's?"

"I hope so."

Later that night, after they made love, Adam continued to hold her, gently stroking her hair.

"My parents have a guest house on their property," he said. "Two bedrooms, plenty of privacy. I'm sure they wouldn't mind having your sister and nieces stay there. Three thousand miles is a hell of a lot more protection than staying at your mom's."

Lena pushed up on an elbow to look at him. "You haven't even met my sister. And your parents are complete strangers. Why would they go out of their way like that?"

"Because you're family," Adam said.

"I'm not—"

"You will be," he said, stroking her belly.

She shivered. "You're crazy."

"Yeah," he whispered, pulling her down for a long open-mouthed kiss that left them both breathless.

~

In the end, Zhanna agreed to the lawyer Lena found, but not to the offer of temporary shelter with Adam's family in Connecticut.

"I can't pull the girls out of school," she told Lena over the phone. "And there are laws. If I take them out of state without Patrick's permission, there might be custody problems later on."

"Sounds like you've looked into it."

"Yeah," Zhanna said. "You wouldn't believe the kinds of things you dream up when you're recovering from a broken rib or a concussion."

"What I can't believe is how you kept it together and hidden for so long."

"Lena—"

"Sorry. No lectures, I promise. Just let me know what I can do to help."

"Thanks," Zhanna said. "I will."

CHAPTER 18

The day before Adam left for his interview in New York, he took Lena grocery shopping.

"I don't understand why we're doing this," she protested, as he pushed the metal cart toward the fresh produce aisle.

"Junior needs more home-cooked food," he said.

Lena rolled her eyes. It had started as a joke, dubbing him Junior after they received Lena's prenatal test results at the start of the week. Forty-six chromosomes, including an XY, and no obvious genetic anomalies. Whatever lingering doubts there might have been about paternity were likewise laid to rest.

"I don't cook," Lena said. "And besides, home-cooked doesn't mean healthy."

"Healthier than take-out every night," he said. "And since I need to expand my repertoire beyond steaks, pasta, and salad, we might as well both learn how to cook."

"I know *how* to cook," she said. "I just don't like to do it."

He slowed down and looked at her. "Really?"

"Yes, really. I like going to the salad bar. And take-out can be healthy, too, if you're careful about what you order."

"Well, we're here now," Adam said. "Let's at least stock up on the basics. When I get back, I'll talk to Mrs. Young about adding some hours."

"Mrs. Young...?"

"My housekeeper."

"I know." Lena hadn't met the woman yet, because she came twice a week in the middle of the day, when Lena was in clinic or at the hospital. But she'd seen evidence of Mrs. Young's work. Freshly laundered linen, tucked in at the corners in a way Lena herself had neither the time nor patience to replicate. Clean dishes, unloaded from the dishwasher and stacked neatly back in the cabinets. Hardwood floors and furniture gleaming with fresh polish. "Why would you need more hours?"

"She mentioned she's a good cook," he said. "I didn't ask her to do it before, but...well, we're both busy and we need to eat. And we'll need a lot more help around the house once Junior's born."

"I was planning on getting a nanny."

"Of course," he agreed. "But that's for Junior. Mrs. Young is for us."

There it was again. *Us.* That tiny, terrifying word that kept cropping up. They had yet to sit down and talk about their future. All Lena knew was that Adam was flying off, and she was staying behind, because she hadn't been able to arrange coverage on such short notice. Or rather, after taking a close look at Erik's haggard face last week, she'd decided not to ask.

Adam had mentioned in passing that he'd look into the possibility of changing venues for his last rotation in order to remain in Los Angeles through the end of her pregnancy. Apparently he expected to attend Junior's birth.

But after that? She had no idea.

While Adam kept saying *us*, as if their status as a couple was assured, Lena needed more than a nebulous two-letter pronoun. She needed to make concrete plans.

Like figuring out where to live. Her apartment in Venice wouldn't do. Located near a busy intersection, it boasted easy access to a half-dozen bars, as well as a tattoo parlor, liquor store, adult toy shop, and marijuana dispensary. What it didn't have was a neighborhood park or library. Fine for a single professional who spent most of her time at work, and colorful enough to attract tons of tourists, but less than ideal for raising a child.

Adam's place wasn't an option either, since it was only available through mid-May, when the owner was returning from a sabbatical abroad.

Which meant Lena had to start looking. Considering Los Angeles real estate prices and rents, it might take a while to find a suitable place that wouldn't land her in bankruptcy court.

She'd have to upgrade her car, too. Something bigger and safer than the junker she'd bought second hand in residency and was still driving. It got her from home to work and back without stalling and managed to squeak by the periodic smog inspections mandated by the state, so until now she hadn't had a good reason to trade it in for something more upscale. But with Junior due in six months, she needed to look into getting a minivan or SUV, or at least a four door sedan with automated safety features that her current car lacked.

And preschool. Rachel, who was just entering her third trimester, was already on three waiting lists.

"You need to sign up practically the moment you find out you're pregnant," Rachel told her yesterday, when they'd finally managed to get together for a celebratory girls' night out. "You know Max Palmer? He and his wife had to wait two years before they finally got in to their top choice."

"But...that's crazy," Lena said.

"Welcome to the Westside," Rachel laughed. "If you thought getting into med school was tough, that's nothing compared to getting your child into the right preschool."

As if Lena didn't have enough to worry about.

"How do you feel about Brussels sprouts?" Adam said.

From the way he was looking at her, this wasn't the first time he'd asked the question.

She wrinkled her nose. "Yuck."

Adam grinned. "Green beans? Broccolini?"

"Okay."

"Want to get started on the fruits while I finish up here?"

"Sure." Keeping her hands busy might help to keep her mounting anxiety at bay. She ripped a plastic bag from an overhead dispenser and headed for the apples.

CHAPTER 19

Adam slipped through a side door into the hotel ballroom. He'd missed most of the talks already, but he wasn't here for the CME. He wasn't supposed to be here at all, was in fact still supposed to be on the East coast, visiting his family.

But after the career-changing decision he'd come to yesterday, he needed to see Lena. Needed to hold her, to remind himself of *why* he'd chucked years of careful preparation out the window. Why he'd chosen to sacrifice a promising career in academic medicine in favor of remaining at a small community hospital where he wasn't even guaranteed a job.

He scanned the room as he moved quietly along the wall. Most of the tables were occupied. He recognized a few faces in profile—surgeons he'd operated with at St. Mary's, several other specialists he'd come to know while doing consults in the ER or rounding on his post-op patients.

There was Rachel, Erik's wife and Lena's best friend, sitting near the front, her hands resting on her prominent bump. Beside her sat a bored-looking Wolf Knox, the wise-cracking hospitalist who'd co-managed several of Adam's patients.

The speaker, an auburn-haired woman in a button-down white shirt and thin pencil skirt, stood beside the podium, her voice rising as she made a point. An older man in a suit and bow tie watched from behind the podium, nodding every few sentences, until someone from the audience tossed him a question and he embarked on a long, rambling answer.

Adam made another visual sweep of the room. He could have sworn Lena mentioned she'd be here today. Unless she'd decided to skip out at the last minute?

But no. There she was, at a table along the opposite wall, her attention fully focused on the speaker.

Adam stood without moving, drinking in the sight of her. She wore a black T-shirt and jeans, her dark hair pinned up in a twist that he couldn't wait to undo.

The last few nights he'd dreamt of those silky strands wrapping around his hands and wrists as Lena bent over his prone body, her naked legs straddling his hips, her bare breasts swaying as she rode him. He'd woken up gasping, alone, the sheets tangled around him, the damp spot a testament to the power of wet dreams.

But it wasn't just the dreams that had him scrambling out of bed in the middle of the night and haphazardly tossing his clothes in a suitcase. It was the slight niggle of doubt that crept in and took root after he'd shared the news with his family.

They'd greeted his announcement with stunned silence, then an avalanche of objections and entreaties to reconsider.

A medical degree with a background in oncology might come in handy, they conceded, especially now that Sterling Therapeutics was expanding into the lucrative business of cancer immunotherapy. But once Adam had gotten his fill of playing doctor in La-La Land, they expected him to return to the family fold and assume his responsibilities.

Sterlings are captains of industry, his father said. Not academics whose careers depended on the vagaries of government funding, or clinicians whose patients could just as easily find care in some other doctor's office.

His father had a seat reserved for Adam on the board of Sterling Therapeutics, and he could walk right into a cushy position as Vice President of research and development.

As for his mother—good God, insanity must run in his family. How could he have missed that all these years? His mother actually had a bride all picked out. The daughter of a lifelong friend, who'd graduated from Smith and volunteered her time to raise money for the same charities her family had supported for generations.

His sister Liz offered him a sympathetic smile but didn't say anything. Amanda was the only one who congratulated him on his impending fatherhood, and promised to visit him in L.A. after she recovered from her own delivery.

With that kind of reception, it was a miracle he hadn't lain awake the entire night, second-guessing himself. He'd actually managed a couple hours of sleep before waking up in a panic at the thought of losing the woman who haunted his dreams.

And so he dressed and packed and caught an Uber to the airport, where he waited on standby for the first available seat on a flight back to LAX.

Now, watching Lena across the room, Adam felt his tension ease.

He imagined her face lighting up when he told her the news. Those soft lips would part, and she'd wrap her arms around him.

"I love you," she'd say.

And then…

The audience broke into applause, startling him out of his fantasy.

People started to get up and gather their belongings. The swell of chatter rose, drowning out the noise of chairs scraping along the floor.

He headed for Lena's table, briefly losing sight of her as he wove through the crowd. The table was empty by the time he got there. He swung around, looking for her, pulse accelerating with each second that he failed to find her.

"Adam?"

Rachel stood at his elbow, a slight frown creasing her forehead.

"I'm looking for Lena," he said. "She was just here…"

"She might have ducked out to the restroom. Through there." Rachel nodded toward a nearby door. "We were sitting together earlier, but then I had to introduce one of the speakers—"

"Thanks," Adam interrupted, and hurried toward the door she'd pointed out.

The line to the ladies' room snaked out into the hallway. He scanned it, then fished out his phone and found an out-of-the-way spot with a view of the restroom door.

Lena picked up on the third ring. "Adam. Hi. How's New York?"

In the background, he could heard traffic noises. "I'll tell you all about it in person," he said. "Where are you?"

"At the Postgraduate Assembly. They just let out."

"I know. I'm standing outside the women's restroom. Where are you?"

A beat of silence, then: "You're back? In L.A.? What happened? Wait—" There was a muffled exchange of words on the other end before she returned. "I'm outside the hotel, at the valet stand. They're bringing my car around. Did you drive?"

"No. I could use a ride." He was already striding down the hall, toward the hotel entrance. Clusters of conference attendees stood around, chatting. He skirted around them, bumped into someone, apologized, and continued winding his way through the growing crowd.

She was standing on the sidewalk, her back to him, digging through her shoulder bag.

"Lose something?" he said, coming up behind her.

She half turned into his arms, and the bag slipped from her fingers. "Adam—"

His mouth covered hers, cutting off the rest of her words. She didn't seem to mind. Her arms twined around his neck as he lifted her off the ground, the momentum making him stagger back a step before he regained his balance and planted both feet firmly on the ground.

She tasted of raspberries and chocolate, sweet and tart and

lush, tantalizing his palate and making him crave more. The kiss went on and on, and might have continued even longer if not for the cacophony of voices and laughter that finally penetrated his sensual fog. Slowly he pulled back, letting her slide down his overheated body until she stood on unstable legs, breathing hard, blinking up at him in the shimmering afternoon heat.

She licked her swollen lips. "Hi."

"Miss me?" he said.

"Yes."

Something in him lightened at the admission. "Maybe I should go away more often."

She let out a shaky laugh and glanced around. Her color deepened when she saw how much attention they'd garnered.

Adam half expected her to back away and pretend to an indifference that neither of them felt, and that no one who'd witnessed their embrace would believe.

But Lena surprised him. She picked up her bag and shouldered it, then wrapped her arm around his and lifted her chin.

"I couldn't find any small bills to tip the valet," she said. "Could you…?"

He grinned. "Sure. Want me to drive?"

She nodded, surprising him again. "Please."

~

At Lena's request, they stopped to eat at a Greek café on the way home. She'd passed on lunch at the conference earlier in favor of a walk down to the beach and back, and now she was starving.

"How was your trip?" she asked after the waiter brought water and took their orders.

Adam didn't answer immediately. "Okay, I guess. I met some people, gave a good talk."

Lena watched for several seconds as he fiddled with the wrapper from his straw, tying evenly spaced knots until he ran out of paper.

"You think they'll make you an offer?" she asked.

He set aside the wrapper and braced his arms on the table. "They did. I turned them down."

"*What?*"

"I've decided to stay here, in L.A. How do you feel about taking on a partner?"

Her eyes widened. "Are you serious?"

"Obviously you'll have to talk it over with Erik," he said. "But it seems a shame to invest so much time and effort in training someone, then releasing him into the wild, don't you think?"

She stared at him, then slowly nodded. "It does seem like a waste."

"I'm officially done in June, but I'll be able to moonlight before then. So don't worry, I'll cover your patients while you're out on maternity leave."

Maternity leave? The thought hadn't even occurred to her. She'd been too busy worrying about other things.

But Adam was right. In less than six months, they were going to be parents. She was going to be a mother. She'd need someone to cover her practice for at least a few weeks while she recovered. But...*Adam?*

She pictured him the way he'd been that first day in her office, sprawled casually in the visitor's chair, a cocky smile on his lips. His voice, a deep rumble that stirred both her libido and her anger: *If I never see another pilonidal cyst in my life,* he'd said, *that's fine by me.*

Surely that wasn't the same person as the slightly rumpled, earnest-looking man sitting across from her now?

The two images blurred. She blinked, disoriented.

"Lena?"

She gripped the edge of the table. It felt solid beneath her fingers. She focused on Adam again, and this time she saw him clearly.

He'd never looked better to her than at this very moment, despite the day-old stubble peppering his cheeks and jaw, and the dark smudges beneath his eyes, and the misbuttoned shirt that probably hadn't seen an iron in years.

"You do realize that you'll be doing pilonidal cysts and appys and all those bread-and-butter things that general surgeons do?"

"I know," he said with a crooked grin. "I don't expect any special treatment. But I'm sure I can build up a reasonable surgical oncology practice over time, given the right incentive..."

A smile tugged at her lips. "Like the prospect of a partnership?"

"For example."

She glanced up as their waiter returned, bearing platters of grilled chicken and lamb kebobs and an assortment of salads.

"I'll talk with Erik," she promised.

They ate in silence for a while.

Adam offered her the pita basket before helping himself. "How's your sister?"

"Hanging in there, I guess." Lena took a sip of water. "Patrick—her husband—keeps calling. Apologizing. Trying to convince her to come back."

Adam frowned. "She's not going to do that, is she?"

"I hope not," Lena sighed. "She has an appointment with a lawyer. My mom's going with her."

"Good."

Lena nodded and changed the subject. "Did you get a chance to see your parents?"

"Yes." He stabbed a piece of lamb with his fork. "My sister Amanda is thrilled for us. She asked for your number, by the way. I hope you don't mind."

"This is the sister who tried to set you up with her friend?"

His dimples flashed. "Yeah, but try not to hold it against her. She's really great, and has tons of experience with kids. Did I tell you she's expecting her fourth around Thanksgiving? Between my sisters and yours, Junior will have plenty of cousins to hang out with."

Lena took a deep breath and let it out slowly.

Three months ago she'd barely begun contemplating the idea of having a child via anonymous sperm donor. Now she was pregnant, and the baby's father was not only planning to stay in the picture, he was also expanding that picture to include a whole slew of his relatives.

"Hey," Adam said, reaching across the table. "Are you okay?"

"Oh, sure," she said. "Never better."

CHAPTER 20

"What's up with you and Dr. McHottie?" Rachel asked.

Lena looked up from her contemplation of the salad bar options in the hospital cafeteria. Her friend rested a tray piled with food on the counter beside her.

It was Monday, two days after she and Adam had made a spectacle of themselves outside the hotel filled with her colleagues. If Lena had harbored any doubts about the efficiency of St. Mary's rumor mill, Rachel's words put those doubts to rest.

"Let's get a table," Lena said.

Over lunch, she told Rachel the news. "Adam's staying in L.A. His sublet expires in a few months, so we're looking for a new lease. Hopefully something bigger than my place."

"Wow, that's great," Rachel said. "When's the wedding?"

"What wedding?" Lena said. "I didn't say anything about a wedding."

"But you're moving in together and having a kid…"

Lena speared a tomato slice. "So? This is the twenty-first century. People don't get married just because they're having a kid together."

Rachel frowned. "Maybe other people don't, but—"

"Look, this isn't exactly a conventional relationship, okay?

Adam's eight years younger than me. His family's…well, let's just say they're not too thrilled about the situation."

Not that Adam had come right out and said it. But Lena wasn't stupid. When the topic of his visit home came up, he'd carefully avoided all mention of his parents. And his sister's endorsement sounded a little suspect too, considering that just a couple months ago Amanda had been all gung-ho about setting him up with someone else.

Lena picked at her salad, wishing yet again that she hadn't indulged her curiosity last night by looking up Adam's family online.

Sure, he'd mentioned growing up with nannies and housekeepers. At the time, Lena hadn't thought much of it, other than feeling sorry for Adam over how little parental attention he had gotten as a child. Many of Lena's friends and colleagues employed nannies and housekeepers. That's what happened in dual-income families where both parents worked demanding jobs.

But according to Google, the Sterlings of Westport, Connecticut were a breed apart. What Adam had so breezily called "the family business" was one of the largest privately-held pharmaceutical companies in the U.S. From its inauspicious start as a small chemical manufacturing plant founded by Adam's grandfather during World War Two, Sterling Therapeutics grew into a multi-billion dollar conglomerate that specialized in the production of antibiotics and antivirals. More recently, under the direction of Adam's father, the company had expanded into biologics and immunotherapy, and was conducting cutting-edge research in the emerging field of immuno-oncology.

Forbes regularly ranked John Sterling near the top of its list of the 400 wealthiest Americans. No wonder Adam had insisted on a paternity test. He'd probably been the target of fortune hunters since he was old enough to shave.

What amazed Lena was how down-to-earth and casual Adam seemed about his background. If she hadn't looked him up, she would never have guessed that he stood to inherit billions. If she hadn't stumbled across pictures of a younger Adam escorting this or that heiress to some celebrity wedding or fundraising gala, she wouldn't have wondered: *what does he see in me?*

And putting aside her own insecurities, there was still the mystery of why Adam, heir to a pharmaceutical empire, would put himself through the misery of medical school and years of residency and fellowship training. What did he have to gain by working so hard?

For Lena, the rewards were obvious. Medicine wasn't just an intellectual challenge, it was also the means to a better life. Becoming a doctor meant she'd finally attain the financial security that had eluded her mother during all those years of struggling to raise two children alone.

Adam already had the world at his fingertips. So what was his motivation? Was he simply trying to prove to himself that he could make it without the support of his family's resources? Or was it a bid for attention—or, worse yet, some grand "fuck you" gesture to the parents who'd outsourced his upbringing? Could the man she'd come to know these last few months truly be that shallow?

No. Of course not.

They'd worked together, eaten together, slept together. Made a child together. He'd cooked for her and cleaned up after her when she was sick. He'd taken her mother's abrasive attitude in stride and offered refuge to Lena's sister and nieces.

He'd infiltrated Lena's world so thoroughly that she couldn't imagine her life without him.

Oh, God.

"Lena?" Rachel's voice pulled her back to the moment. "I have to get back to the ER. I'll call you later, okay? Tonight, after work. I want details."

Details Lena and Adam had yet to work out.

Lena gave her friend a weak nod and took a deep breath, trying to quell her rising sense of panic.

~

The first cramp hit as she was finishing up a laparascopic cholecystectomy. Lena sucked in a sharp breath, her hands stilling for a moment. The nurse practitioner who was assisting looked inquiringly at her from across the table.

Lena gritted her teeth and ignored the look. "I don't see any more bleeders. Let's get the trocars out and close."

By the time the final counts were completed and the patient was ready for transfer to the PACU, Lena was drenched in sweat. The cramps were coming on top of one another now. She tore off her sterile gown and gloves and rushed to the locker room.

But she knew, even before she felt the gush of fluid and saw the blood staining her scrubs, that it was over.

CHAPTER 21

Adam tore down the stairs and past the startled guard at the entrance to the ER.

He spotted Rachel at first nurses' station. "Where is she?"

"Room four. Wait—" Rachel grabbed his arm. "She doesn't know I called you. She didn't want anyone there."

Even though that was typical Lena, the words still stung. "How is she?"

"We gave her Toradol for the pain. She's resting. She'll probably be able to go home soon."

Adam hesitated. "The baby?"

Rachel shook her head. "I'm sorry."

Adam nodded and let out a shuddering breath. "Thanks."

He entered the room. Lena looked washed out, like the thin hospital blanket that covered her half-reclining form.

She opened her eyes as he approached the bed. "You heard."

"Yes." He snagged a chair and sat down beside her. Her hand felt cold and limp between his own. "I'm so sorry."

She closed her eyes again. For several minutes they sat in silence, not moving.

Eventually Lena stirred, opened her eyes, and pulled her hand away. "The D&C's scheduled for tomorrow."

"I'll take you."

"No." The word came out sharply, like a slap.

He frowned. "You'll need help…"

"Rachel can come with me."

Adam sighed and ran a hand through his hair. There was no tactful way of saying this. "Sweetheart, Rachel is six months pregnant with twins. The last thing either of you needs is for her to go with you for your D&C."

Lena's fingers tightened on the blanket. "Fine. I'll ask my mom."

"Lena—"

"No," she said, cutting him off. "The baby's gone. You're off the hook. Free to leave. So go. Just. Go."

"You don't mean that." He leaned closer. "Please—"

"You didn't want this," she said. "You said it yourself, you weren't ready. Well, you got your wish. There's no baby. Nothing to keep you here."

"Except you, Lena." He reached for her hand again, gripping it firmly until she stopped trying to pull away. "I'm not going anywhere without you. Okay? I'll take you for the procedure tomorrow, and then we'll go home and you'll rest and we'll talk. Maybe Dr. Goodman can suggest a good therapist or support group or something."

"I don't need a therapist or support group."

"It might help to lean on someone else for a change. Please," he said again. "Don't shut me out. We're in this together. We'll get through it together."

"The only reason we were together is because I got pregnant."

"No, Lena. You got pregnant because we were together."

She stared at their joined hands. "We weren't *together*. We hooked up. There's a difference."

"I know there's a difference," he said. "And maybe you're right, maybe that's how it started. But things changed. Our relationship changed."

"No—"

"Yes," he said. "It did, Lena. We started building a life

together. We *are* building a life together. Here, in L.A. We have an appointment with a real estate agent. I'm joining you and Erik in practice."

"You had your heart set on Sloan Kettering."

"My head, maybe," he said. "But not my heart. My heart is right here, with you. I love you, Lena. And that's not going to change. No matter what happens, I love you."

Her lip trembled, and he held his breath, waiting for her to say something. But all she did was bite her lip and look away.

He swallowed and forged on. "I'm sorry about the baby. I'm sorry you're in pain. But we'll get through this, I promise. And we'll have other kids."

"No," she said, her voice barely a whisper.

"Yes."

She shook her head and used her free hand to wipe her eyes. "I'm turning forty in January. The odds of my getting pregnant again and carrying a pregnancy to term—"

"Screw the odds," he said. "We'll figure it out. If we need to, we'll do assisted reproduction, or use a surrogate, or adopt."

"But…why?" She turned back to him, brows drawn. "You could have anyone."

"So could you," he said. "But you're the only woman I want, Lena. I love you."

He waited for a few seconds while she continued to stare at him, then prompted, "This would be the part where you tell me how you feel."

She licked her lips. "I…" Her voice faltered and she looked away. "I…don't know."

He let out a slow breath and nodded. Who knew that such innocuous sounding words could wound so deeply?

He managed to find his voice. "Fair enough," he said. "We'll take it one step at a time. Get through tomorrow first. And the day after that. And then maybe once you're feeling a little better, we can readdress the question."

Because he wasn't giving up on her. On them.

She sighed and closed her eyes. "Thank you."

~

Either Mrs. Young didn't have the extra time to spare, or Adam never asked her to take over the cooking. Lena didn't know, and didn't ask. The result was the same, regardless.

Adam ordered a half dozen colorful cookbooks with step-by-step instructions that he had Lena read aloud to him while he chopped and sautéed, mixed and seasoned his way through Central and South America, then China and the Indian subcontinent.

After months of nothing but bland food, the exotic spices exploded on Lena's tongue, making her eyes water. Or at least that's what she claimed when Adam silently nudged the tissue box closer.

Each evening over dinner, he worked on keeping the conversation light. Lena found herself tuning out the words, just listening to the tenor of his voice. Watching his lips move and his eyes crinkle when he told an amusing story. Following the movement of his strong, capable hands as he gestured to illustrate a point.

"Did I ever tell you how I got to be a doctor?" he asked one evening as they were clearing up after dinner.

She looked up from the dishes she was washing. "I assume you went to medical school, like everyone else."

"Well, yes," he said. "But before that. I was supposed to join the family business, like every other Sterling since Gramps founded the company."

She shut off the water. "So what happened?"

"I broke my leg skiing when I was in junior high. Classic tib-fib fracture." He smiled and leaned against the counter. "The orthopedist who did my surgery was amazing. She was probably just a couple years out of residency, and my parents wanted someone more experienced. But it was Christmas, and she was the one on call, and it turned out to be the best thing that could have happened to me."

"Breaking a leg?"

He shook his head. "Falling in love. I decided then and there that I wanted to be a doctor."

"Wait a minute." She tore off a paper towel and dried her hands in stiff, jerky movements. "You went into medicine because of a stupid teenage crush?"

"Hey, that's my ego you're trampling on," he said. "And no, I didn't go into medicine because of a crush. I got over that pretty quickly. But the experience did get me thinking, and all of a sudden I realized that there was an entire world of possibilities out there that didn't include Sterling Therapeutics."

"What did your parents say?"

He shrugged. "They thought I'd change my mind. Halfway through med school, I guess it dawned on them that I was serious. My dad took me aside and asked if I really wanted to spend the rest of my life in drudgery."

Lena's mouth fell open. "You're kidding."

"Nope, those were his exact words. And he still tells me every so often that there's a place for me at Sterling Therapeutics, anytime I want to quit medicine."

She studied his expression. "You're not quitting."

It wasn't a question, but he answered anyway. "Not in this lifetime. You want to know why?"

"Because you're stubborn?"

His lips quirked. "Yeah. Plus, I love what I do."

At night, they slept in the same bed without making love. She relaxed only when she felt the comforting weight of his arms wrap around her, his breath a soothing lullaby that pulled her into sleep.

They didn't talk about the baby, or the miscarriage, or the future.

There was just the perpetual present, and Lena would have been content to drift that way from one day to the next, barely registering anything outside the protected bubble she and Adam had created.

Until early one Friday evening, when the bubble burst, and reality came rushing in.

She was on call, examining a patient in the ER, when an overhead announcement pierced her concentration.

"Code gray, Emergency Room. Code gray, Emergency Room."

Out in the hallway, a man was shouting obscenities. His voice abruptly cut off as something crashed, and then there was a cacophony of raised voices and the sound of running feet.

Lena excused herself and rushed to the sliding glass door on the other side of the privacy curtain. Her view was obstructed by a small crowd of medical personnel.

She slipped out the door into the hall.

"What's going on?" she asked a scrub-clad nurse who stood at the edge of the crowd.

"Some guy threatened Dr. Harding," the nurse said. "But she's okay."

She...? Oh, God, *Rachel* Harding, not Erik. Rachel, who was almost seven months pregnant. Lena felt the blood drain from her face.

"Dr. Knox took the guy down," the nurse continued. "Before anyone else could move. *Bam.* Like Bruce Lee. One kick."

"Rachel—Dr. Harding—" Lena interrupted. "Where is she?"

"Oh, she got out of the way, soon as Dr. Knox took over." The nurse fanned herself with her hand. "I tell you, that man is *fine.* He can take me down anytime he wants to."

Two uniformed security guards rushed by and pushed their way through the crowd. Outside, Lena heard the wail of approaching police sirens.

People started to disperse, slowly drifting back to their work stations when the police arrived and took over.

As the area cleared, Lena could see the man at the center of the fray. He lay sprawled face-down on the floor some thirty feet away, still writhing and spewing obscenities, even as the police handcuffed him and hauled him out of the ER through the double doors to the ambulance bay. Two officers stayed behind to gather information.

It took a minute for Lena to spot Rachel behind one of the nurses' stations, her ashen face framed by a frizzier-than-usual mop of black hair. A nurse hovered over her, while Max Palmer, one of the other ER doctors, crouched beside her, measuring her blood pressure.

Why? Was she hurt? The nurse who'd filled Lena in earlier said Rachel was okay, but what if she wasn't? What if the stress of the altercation led to complications with her pregnancy? What if—

No. No. No.

Nothing was going to happen. Max Palmer was right there, with Rachel. She was in good hands. Max knew what he was doing. If anything happened—

Lena tried to block out all the terrible possibilities. Premature labor. Pre-eclampsia. Placental abruption.

Stop.

Rachel was strong. Her twins were healthy. Everything would be fine.

Just because Lena's pregnancy had ended in miscarriage didn't mean Rachel's would.

Their situations were completely different.

Rachel was much farther along in her pregnancy than Lena had been.

Rachel had a husband who loved her, who'd support her no matter what happened. While Lena had...

What? What did she have?

She closed her eyes and took a deep breath, willing her pulse to slow.

Adam.

She had Adam. Adam, who loved her, and supported her through the bleakest experience of her life, even though she'd repeatedly tried to push him away. And he continued to stand by her, despite the fact that she'd given him no encouragement and had refused to acknowledge even to herself how much he meant to her.

But the feeling was there, strong and true and undeniable.

Love.

She loved him.

Lena opened her eyes and glanced toward Rachel. Max was now standing, patting Rachel on the shoulder. Wait, where was he going? Didn't he realize Rachel shouldn't be left alone?

Lena started across the hall, toward the nurses' station, then stopped abruptly and glanced over her shoulder at the half-closed door she'd left behind.

Crap. Her patient was still waiting. Assuming his CT scan showed no surprises, she'd recommend a trial of IV antibiotics and bowel rest for a few days, then base further treatment on his response. The man might still end up in the OR, but not tonight.

She shot another glance at Rachel, who was now sitting alone, eyes half-closed, hands resting on her burgeoning belly. What was she feeling? Were the babies moving?

Lena reached for her phone. Should she call Rachel's obstetrician first, then Erik? Or...

Wait, what was this? A disheveled-looking Wolf Knox rounded the nurses' station and dropped into a chair beside Rachel. They exchanged a few words, and Rachel laughed.

Lena felt her own lips turn up in the ghost of a smile. Trust Wolf to lighten an impossibly tense situation.

As Lena watched, Rachel and Wolf continued to talk, ignoring the activity around them.

Ten minutes, that's all Lena needed to wrap up her consult and enter the appropriate orders into the patient's chart. Surely she could count on Wolf to stick around that long? Ten minutes. Then she'd check on Rachel herself.

And once she made sure that Rachel was fine and safely back in Erik's care, Lena would head home.

Straight into Adam's arms.

EPILOGUE

Three years later...

"Slow down," Adam said.

Lena blew a wisp of hair out of her eyes. "I can't," she said, checking the supply of spare toiletries in the guest bathroom downstairs. "Your family will be here any minute. Amanda texted and said they're on their way. And my mother's still in the dining room, holding Mrs. Young hostage."

"What are they arguing about now?"

"The place settings," Lena huffed, straightening up. "I mean, seriously, do you care if the dessert spoon faces left or right?"

"Not particularly." Adam stepped closer.

Their eyes met in the mirror she felt a familiar flutter in her chest. Nearly three-and-a-half years together, and she still couldn't believe how lucky she was, or how close she'd come to throwing it all away.

He wrapped his arms around her from behind. For a moment she allowed herself to relax and lean against him. His hands settled on her massive belly just in time to catch the ripple of a tiny foot or elbow beneath his palm.

"Active little bugger," he murmured.

"Takes after his dad."

He smiled and kissed her temple. "Maybe you should go lie down. Get some rest."

"Can't," she sighed. "There's still a ton of things to do." She pulled away.

Adam followed her out of the bathroom and down the hall. "The caterers have it all under control."

"You told them we need another seat at the table?"

"Yes."

"I still can't believe Zhanna waited until the last minute to tell us. It was already a tight squeeze—"

"It's fine," Adam said. "And he seems nice enough."

Lena didn't respond. Patrick had seemed nice, too. Initially.

Was she being too critical? Her sister deserved some happiness. She'd floundered for over a year after an ugly divorce, then finally pulled herself together, completed her undergraduate degree online, and enrolled in a masters program in clinical psychology. Which was how she'd met the man she was bringing to dinner.

Their mother was thrilled, of course. So what if he was fourteen years older than Zhanna, twice-divorced, and had two grown children of his own? He was a *professor*! And he'd waited until Zhanna was no longer his student before approaching her—didn't that prove he was a decent, respectable man?

Lena glanced into the dining room, where her mother and Mrs. Young were still squabbling. The housekeeper was well-paid, but after tonight they'd owe her a huge bonus.

In the kitchen, Lena paused and took a breath. The temperature was at least a few degrees higher here, despite the fact that the back door was open. Uniformed staff streamed in and out to the accompaniment of rapid-fire Spanish and the clanging of cookware. An oven timer went off. The refrigerator door slammed. Everywhere she looked, there was a blur of activity. Trays were unloaded, ingredients prepped, steaming pots were ferried from stove to sink.

"See?" Adam said. "They're on top of it. Let's get out of

the way."

He steered her out the back door, past the temporary bar that was being set up on the patio, and toward the gazebo.

Lena balked. "Adam, I don't have time for this. Your parents—"

"Are looking forward to spending time with us," he said. "Stop worrying. Everything will be fine."

Easy for him to say. Despite two-and-a-half years of marriage, Lena still felt on shaky ground with Adam's parents.

"They're a little reserved," Adam conceded the first time she'd flown with him to the East coast for a traditional Sterling family Thanksgiving.

Try encased in ice, she thought, watching his mother exchange air kisses while his father stared impassively from a distance.

Lena had been three months pregnant with the twins at the time. Dr. Goodman assured her that the pregnancy was progressing normally, but she remained anxious—or, as Adam put it, in a heightened state of vigilance—for the next five months. It was only when she heard two robust cries in the OR while Dr. Goodman was still suturing her up that she was finally able to relax.

But during that first Thanksgiving at the Sterling family compound in Westport, Connecticut, Lena suffered in silence. Her new in-laws hadn't known about the pregnancy yet, nor about the difficulties she and Adam had encountered getting pregnant after her first miscarriage.

As far as they were concerned, Lena was still a temporary presence in their son's life. Adam's mother drove that point home by introducing Lena to the daughter of her long-time friend. *This is Anabelle, dear*, she'd said. *Anabelle and Adam grew up together, and were always such good friends. Why don't we leave them to catch up while I introduce you to Adam's cousin…*

Luckily Adam had rescued her minutes later, and spent the rest of the night glued to her side, despite the dark looks his mother threw their way.

The following year was an improvement. They arrived with the five-month-old twins in tow, and even Adam's mother couldn't resist their gummy smiles for long.

This year, Adam announced they'd be hosting Thanksgiving in California, in deference to Lena's advanced stage of pregnancy. Dr. Goodman admonished her against flying, unless she wanted to deliver without an epidural at thirty-six thousand feet. So they stayed at home. With the support of his sisters, Adam convinced his parents to take a break from tradition, and fly out to L.A. for a week.

He sweetened the deal by offering to help his dad scout out possible locations for a new West coast office for Sterling Therapeutics. The man obviously hadn't given up on the idea of luring Adam back into the fold with a plum position in the family business, though Adam seemed quite happy with his current situation.

And why not? He'd transformed their practice from a small general surgery office into a thriving multi-specialty group.

Lena had doubts when he'd first proposed the partnership arrangement. Even more so later, after Erik's unexpected death left Lena—along with the entire medical staff of St. Mary's—feeling shaken and confused. The hospital administration brought in an expert to discuss physician burnout and depression, though that did little to ease Lena's guilt over the loss of her long-time friend and mentor.

It was Adam who kept the practice going while Lena grieved. Adam who convinced her that she owed it to herself and her patients to carry on. Adam who helped rebuild her confidence and pointed out the benefits of recruiting new doctors to share the workload and expand the practice.

They started with a young general surgeon fresh out of residency, then a breast surgeon who'd grown frustrated with the bureaucracy at her large academic institution. A plastic reconstructive surgeon followed, then an endocrine surgeon, urogynecologist, colorectal surgeon, and thoracic surgeon.

"Diversification," Adam called it. Whatever it was, Lena had to admit it worked.

"Any regrets?" she asked him a few days ago, as they retired early for bed.

Adam raised a brow. "Are you kidding? I've got everything I want right here."

"Really?" She paused in the process of taking down her hair and glanced at him.

"I've got the smartest, most beautiful wife in the world," he said, coming up behind her. "Two amazing kids, and a third on the way." He rested a hand on her belly and bent to kiss her neck. "A great career." Another kiss. "What more could a man possibly want?"

That was the moment their bedroom door burst open and the twins, now nearly eighteen months old, careened into the room, screeching with glee at having temporarily escaped both the nanny and Mrs. Young.

Adam swooped down and caught a squirming bundle in each arm.

"See?" he laughed. "Never a dull moment."

Forty minutes later, with the twins finally asleep, Adam shed his clothes and joined Lena in bed. "Where were we?"

"Discussing what more a man could possibly want."

"Ah." Adam shifted closer, rolling onto his side so he could spoon Lena from behind. "An easy delivery would be nice."

"Very nice," she agreed. "Though you realize, we're never going have any peace and quiet after that?"

"Peace and quiet are overrated," he said, nuzzling his nose into her hair. "I prefer loud and happy."

"Mm," Lena murmured. "Happy is good."

He stroked his fingers down her arm. "So, are you?"

"What?"

"Happy."

"Oh, yes." She smiled and caught his hand, lacing their fingers together. "Very happy."

"Good." He kissed her bare shoulder. "I'll remind you of that in a few days."

"A few days...?" She turned her head to look at him.

He grinned and kissed her again, this time on the mouth, and as the kiss deepened, she forgot all about his promise.

Until a few days later, on Thanksgiving, when Adam led her

to the gazebo out back, and they settled onto a cushioned bench.

"Stop worrying," he said. "Everything will be fine."

"But—"

"I love you." He brushed her lips with his. "And you love me."

She breathed in his familiar scent. Even now, despite her anxiety over his parents' visit, it stirred her senses. "Yes."

"Remember that," he said. "Because that's all that matters. And it won't change, whatever else happens. Okay?"

She took a steadying breath and nodded, just as the distant chimes of the doorbell announced the arrival of their guests.

Adam rose from the bench and looked at her.

"Ready?" he asked, extending his hand to help her up.

She looked into his eyes and smiled. "Ready."

~ The End ~

NOTE FROM THE AUTHOR

Thank you for reading *Oh, Baby!*
I hope you enjoyed Lena and Adam's story.
Reviews are the lifeblood of any author. If you can, please take
a few minutes to post your review of *Oh, Baby!* on Amazon
or Goodreads. It doesn't have to be elaborate – just a line or
two telling others what you thought of the book would be
much appreciated.

Thank you!

LOOKING FOR MORE BY JILL BLAKE?

<u>Prescription: Romance!</u>
Oh, Baby! ~ Lena & Adam
The Burnout Cure ~ Lily & Wolf

<u>The Silicon Beach Trilogy:</u>
Beyond the Ivory Tower (Book 1) ~ Anna & Ethan
Sweet Indulgence (Book 2) ~ Becca & Leo
A Matter of Trust (Book 3) ~ Klara & Vlad

<u>The Santa Monica Trilogy:</u>
Without a Net (Book 1) ~ Eva & Max
Coming Home (Book 2) ~ Grace & Logan
Balancing Act (Book 3) ~ Angie & Zach

<u>The Doctors of Rittenhouse Square Trilogy:</u>
Pursued by the Playboy (Book 1) ~ Kate & Marc
Taking a Chance (Book 2) ~ Samantha & Alex
This Time for Keeps (Book 3) ~ Isabelle & Luca

Turn the page to read more about these titles…

The Burnout Cure
(A Prescription: Romance! Book)

When it comes to burnout, Lily Reid is an expert. Determined to turn her personal tragedy into a cautionary lesson for other physicians, she travels the country, lecturing about life balance and stress management. But her words falls on deaf ears—until she hits on a plan to appeal to a broader audience.

Enter Dr. Wolf Knox, aka "Wolfman MD." He's gorgeous, charismatic, and his patients love him. So do millions of fans who follow him online, watching the music videos he makes in his spare time. Too bad Wolf believes "burnout" is synonymous with weakness. His motto? Suck it up—and if you can't handle the pressure, get the hell out of medicine.

As Lily and Wolf clash over plans for a joint project, their mutual disdain gives way to desire. But when a fellow physician's suicide forces them to confront their own fears and prejudices, will their fledgling relationship survive?

(Please note: This is a steamy contemporary romance that contains mature themes and explicit content, meant for adults 18 and over. It is a stand-alone novel, with no cliff-hangers, and a guaranteed HEA.)

THE SILICON BEACH TRILOGY

Beyond the Ivory Tower *(Book 1)* ~ Anna & Ethan
When venture capitalist Ethan Talbot offers to pay top students to drop out of school, math professor Anna Lazarev goes on the warpath. But their battle over education takes an unexpected turn, thanks to a mutual attraction that's impossible to ignore.

Sweet Indulgence *(Book 2)* ~ Becca & Leo
Leo Kogan has a brilliant medical career, great friends, loving family. All that's missing is the perfect woman: Becca Markham. But going from friends to lovers proves harder than he expects—especially when Becca embarks on a risky business venture that threatens to turn Leo's safe, stable world upside down.

A Matter of Trust *(Book 3)* ~ Klara & Vlad
Venture capitalist Vlad Snezhinsky excels at two things: making money and being a dad. Still struggling through a bitter divorce, he has zero interest in romance—until he meets Klara Lazarev. But when murder throws their world into chaos, can new love survive when it's a matter of trust?

THE SANTA MONICA TRILOGY

Without a Net *(Book 1)* ~ Eva & Max
Betrayed by her husband, single mom to her young son, struggling to keep head above water, the last thing Eva needs is another philandering male. But when her best friend's older brother offers her a job, can Eva resist what may be the biggest adventure of her life?

Coming Home *(Book 2)* ~ Grace & Logan
Eight years after she leaves for New York, scandal sends Grace fleeing home and into the arms of her old college boyfriend. Sometimes, first love deserves a second chance—but can it survive when past secrets and betrayals come to light?

Balancing Act *(Book 3)* ~ Angie & Zach
When Angie goes head to head against her old nemesis Zach, "backroom negotiation" takes on a whole new meaning. As lawyers on opposite sides of a case, they've got plenty to argue about. But legal wrangling takes a backseat when their mutual attraction threatens to spin out of control.

DOCTORS OF RITTENHOUSE SQUARE

Pursued by the Playboy (Book 1) ~ Kate & Marc
A top-notch gynecologist with a playboy reputation, Marc DiStefano is finally looking to settle down. He sets his sights on Kate Warner, a career-driven woman who doesn't believe in love—and that's when the problems begin.

Taking a Chance (Book 2) ~ Samantha & Alex
When burnt-out family physician Samantha Winters trades her big-city career for a rural clinic, she figures it's a temporary gig. Falling for the local golden boy is not on her agenda. Alex Kane spent years building his company and raising his sister's orphaned kids. Now he's ready to cut loose and have some fun. Too bad the new doc isn't interested...or is she?

This Time for Keeps (Book 3) ~ Isabelle & Luca
When a senseless act of violence shatters her perfect world, Dr. Isabelle DiStefano struggles to rebuild: new life, new job, new man. But sometimes the past can be hard to leave behind, especially when old flame Luca Santoro decides he wants her back...this time, for keeps.

ABOUT THE AUTHOR

A native of Philadelphia, Jill Blake now lives in southern California with her husband and three children. By day, she works as a physician in a busy medical practice. By night, she pens steamy romances.

Jill loves hearing from readers! You can contact her through any of the following:

Website: https://www.authorjillblake.com/
Facebook: https://facebook.com/jill.blake.3386
Twitter: https://twitter.com/Jill_Blake_

To sign up for giveaways and get notified when Jill has a new book out, go to http://eepurl.com/UMZZ9.